D0365812

I would have to go to Nika's funeral after all. You see what I mean, don't you? Now I had to see who *wasn't* there.

Do you remember Edie Adams's wonderful line about the wedding of one of LBJ's daughters? "Only the immediate country is invited," she said.

Well, Nika's funeral was like that, standing room only. Either *she* was very, very popular or the fact that she'd departed this earthly realm was. I'd bet on the latter. In fact, Suzie had said that Nika's body wasn't being laid out on display in its coffin because the funeral director didn't want anyone to see the stake he'd had to place through her heart.

Also by Carolyn Banks
Published by Fawcett Books:

THE GIRLS ON THE ROW

DEATH BY DRESSAGE

Carolyn Banks

FAWCETT GOLD MEDAL • NEW YORK

Sale of this book without a front cover may be unauthorized. If this book is coverless, it may have been reported to the publisher as "unsold or destroyed" and neither the author nor the publisher may have received payment for it.

A Fawcett Gold Medal Book
Published by Ballantine Books
Copyright © 1993 by Carolyn Banks

All rights reserved under International and Pan-American Copyright Conventions. Published in the United States of America by Ballantine Books, a division of Random House, Inc., New York, and simultaneously in Canada by Random House of Canada Limited, Tornoto.

Library of Congress Catalog Card Number: 93-90530

ISBN 0-449-14843-2

Manufactured in the United States of America

First Edition: November 1993

This book is dedicated to
the memory of
Phillip Jacob Dogonka,
my father,
a lover of horses.

CHAPTER 1

"Hey, Robin," Ject said. "I think something happened to that friend of yours, what's her name, Veronika."

"Oh, right, let me guess," I hollered from the next room. Nika, as Ject well knew, was no friend of mine. "It was back-alley liposuction, right?" Word was that Nika's husband had cut her off: no more face-lifts, tummy tucks, boob augmentation. Therefore, my remark.

But Jeet appeared in the doorway, looking stern and maybe even shaken. "I mean it," he said. "Come see."

I got up off the floor, where I'd been cleaning my horse's tack, pushing newspapers and saddle soap and neat's-foot oil and my bucket aside. I followed my husband to the television set and we both stared wide-eyed, waiting for the commercials to wind down.

"Seriously, what'd they say? Did they say that she—" But Jeet shooshed me as the five o'clock news came back on.

And sure enough. There was a shot of the big double gate at Cliffside Farm and then a cut to where a section of the barn was all roped off with that yellow crime tape.

"Veronika Ballinger, a prominent Austin woman,"

the news reporter was saying, "was found near death this morning at her posh suburban . . ."

I watched the screen and shivered, especially when they talked about how she died. Apparently Nika had taken an enormous blow to the skull.

And there was Manuel on the screen, explaining in his broken English how he'd come upon his employer's body. "She bleeding," he said poignantly, "but she breathe."

He had called Veronika's husband, Ron, and Ron, presumably, had dialed 911.

"Then," Manuel went on, looking skyward and waving his arm, "helicopter come. . . ."

But Nika had perished after several hours in intensive care.

"Oh, gross," I said. "And we were here, just going about our business, while she—"

Before I could get this out, the front door burst open and my best friend, Lola, all but fell inside. "Did you hear?" she asked. She joined us on the sofa. "God, can you believe?"

She and I started speculating about what might have happened when all of a sudden I noticed that in the background Jeet was dialing the phone.

"Who are you calling?" I asked.

A buddy of his at the paper, he said, and then he kept right on.

Lola and I listened as he asked for Vince, who had the crime beat. After several I-see and Uh-huh-type remarks, Jeet hung up and announced, "They think it was a homicide."

Lo and I gasped in unison. People you know just don't get murdered. Really, it just couldn't be.

"Well," Lola said. "Everybody did kind of hate her guts."

* * *

It was true. Because Veronika Ballinger—Nika, we called her—had been a runaway bitch. Her bitchiness had been very individualized. Like she found out whatever it was that drove you—you, personally—crazy and then did it. It was weird, a power quest, as if rendering a person totally miserable was, for her, a source of nourishment. Her methods, Jeet once said, were as elaborate as the label on a bottle of vermouth.

With me it involved money. Jeet and I always seemed to be poor, but that's another story.

And anyway, what she did to me doesn't seem like anything compared with what she did to other people. Take Lola. Nika had actually seduced Cody Penn, who at the time had been Lola's man. Did I say seduced? That's maybe too mild a term. I mean, Lo and I had actually found Nika *impaled* upon Cody in the parking lot of the restaurant where we'd been celebrating Lola's engagement to the man. Even now, two years after the fact, we didn't talk about the episode. And Cody, fortunately, had the good sense never to be seen again.

"The police'll have a field day with this one," Lola said now. Her voice seemed awfully flat. As though she'd had to work at keeping it that way.

By the ten o'clock news, they had a photo to display, a still of Veronika in formal riding attire—I mean top hat, the long-tailed coat they call a shadbelly, the works—on one of her fancy Warmbloods—you know, breeds like Oldenburg and Hanoverian, big-buck imports, usually. I was just on the verge of registering something important when the news blurb was cut off by an urgent bulletin.

* * *

I awakened to the smell of something wonderful emanating from the kitchen. Not an infrequent occurrence around here. You see, Jeet is the food editor at the *Austin Daily Progress*, which means that all week long he tests recipes for his big schmear in the Wednesday paper. It also means that once a week we eat out so that he can do a restaurant review as well. As Jeet always says, we'll never go hungry.

The paper pays so little, though, that we almost do. But, in fairness, we would probably do okay if I weren't completely hooked on what has to be the most expensive sport there is: riding. And not just riding, but dressage.

What's dressage? The answer isn't simple. It's a search for perfection: for the horse's perfect walk, perfect trot, perfect canter, even perfect halt. Demonstrated while riding the perfect circle, the perfect line. You do—or maybe I should say attempt—all of it within the perfect space, which is to say, the surface is a certain size (twenty by sixty meters, if details like that matter to you) and perfectly flat. What this proves, according to my husband, is that perfection, even the search for it, is boring.

Anyway, I staggered into the kitchen and asked what we were having. Polenta with a salsa fresca, poached egg, with grated jack cheese and slivered avocado for garnish. "Oh, yummy," I said, going heavy on the avocado. "What's the focus?"

"Brunch." Jeet frowned at my plate.

I guess I also ought to tell you that I do battle constantly—I mean constantly—with my weight. Dressage is the only thing that keeps me from just flat out giving up and letting myself become the thousand-pounder I was meant to be. Because in riding breeches—particularly here

in Texas where you hardly ever wear your riding coat—
there's no place for a spare tire to hide. I mean, you come
down that arena centerline *fat*. Want an image to ponder?
Think of Buddha sitting up there in the saddle. Buddha in
an English riding outfit setting out to ride past the judge's
stand. Give me another couple years and I could look like
Buddha, too, because my face is round and my eyes are
round. At the moment I'm a size fourteen, but someday—
and I'm talking soon—I fear I'll be opening a Lane Bryant
charge account.

What really hurts is that just about everybody involved with the sport is a sylph. Which is one thing I
really liked about Veronika. She was definitely, by
nature, not a sylph. She was, in fact, even pudgier
than me.

Oh, she'd go away to fat farms and come *back* a sylph.
But then, in even as little as a month, she'd start ballooning up again.

Well, maybe ballooning isn't the right word. I mean,
I balloon. Nika had a more feminine form of weight
gain. She would just get bustier, hippier, curvier, kind
of like one of those primitive fertility figures. Nonetheless, her battle with the bulge was a source of comfort
to me. Misery loves, etc., even if her weight gain,
wherein she retained her waist, seemed more desirable
than my own version.

But look! How am I supposed to stay thin when I'm
married to a man like Jeet? When he's not making de-
licious things to eat, he's reading about making them.
And half the time he's reading out loud to me.

"Hey, Robin, listen to this," he'll say, looking up
from the *Larousse Gastronomique*. "Doesn't this sound
great?" Then he'll proceed to read the details of some
excruciatingly yummy thing, like parfait amour or va-

nilla meringues with chantilly cream. I think I put on weight just hearing about the stuff.

"This is wonderful," I said now, trying to restrain myself from asking if he'd mind poaching me yet another egg.

"And it's fat free," he said.

"This is?" I pointed.

"Not the avocado, and not the cheese," he said, "but the rest."

"No kidding." I spooned a little more polenta, a little more salsa, onto my plate. "Did you see the late news last night?"

"Barely," Jeet admitted.

"Well, they showed this picture of Nika and she was on this horse. This picture, there was something about it. I mean, I can't quite . . ."

But as soon as I'd mentioned the word *horse*, his eyes had glazed over. He mumbled something about asking Vince for an update when he got in to work and that was that.

All the while I was feeding and haying and fertilizing the water trough and shoveling the manure du jour, I kept thinking about Veronika's picture. Something kept niggling at me, you know the way I mean. Like someone calls you up and asks you who played Batman on TV, and you know but you just can't think of the name? And trying doesn't help. Well, this was like that. I knew, but it wouldn't come, wouldn't come, wouldn't come, and it just kept bothering me.

It bothered me while I scraped the night's accumulation of crud off Plum, my mare, and it bothered me while I waited for her to deflate so that I could tighten her girth. It bothered me while I went through all of the exercises that I use to loosen up her aging musculature before we really get to work.

What I mean is, I get on Plum and, at the walk, let her stretch her head and neck way, way down, taking every bit as much rein as she cares to. Meanwhile, I make sure those back legs keep oomphing right along. Then I do the same at trot and, on really good days, at canter as well.

It sounds stupid, but it gives me a thrill to do these things with Plum. When I got her—nine years ago—she was a racetrack reject. This meant she ran away with me at any and every opportunity, only not quite as fast as the previous owner had hoped. Anyway, I tried all kinds of gadgetry, all kinds of medieval-looking things that were supposed to hold her in check. Then someone said, "Have you tried dressage?" I mean, why not? I was at that point considering the guillotine, so why not dressage, which is really just a systematic training method? And so now, here was the formerly crazy Plum, working just as calm and cool as could be. Plum, on a long rein, being trustworthy.

Of course that isn't all we do. I do eventually gather her up and make her do some work. Some days we concentrate on little things, like sharpening her canter departs. Other days we actually ride some of the tests from the shows. We do the latter especially if there's one—a show, that is—coming up.

And maybe it sounds Californian, but I do a lot of visualization, too. In my mind's eye I see myself, not in my *Manure Movers of America* shirt and my rattiest breeches, but in full regalia: white breeches, white gloves, a stock tie, a derby. And since all of this is in my head, I become a little taller and a little thinner besides.

Boots gleaming, I turn down the centerline and . . .

As a result of this seemingly idle musing, what I'd been reaching for came to me. What I'd been trying to figure out about that picture of Nika on TV: Nika's outfit was all wrong for the level she'd been riding. It was the kind of getup that you wear when you show FEI, which is to say in the upper-upper echelons of the sport. FEI, for those of you who want to know *everything*, actually means "Fédération Equestre Internationale," except that people use it to mean just what I said: upper-upper echelons of the sport. The sport goes from training level to first, second, third, fourth, fifth. *Then* the FEI levels begin, so you can see how upper-upper I mean. Anyway, Nika had never ridden—and I doubted that even if she'd lived to be a hundred, she would ever have ridden—above second. Even first level, for her, was a strain.

For the truth was, no matter how much Nika spent on lessons alone (and she did spend probably more than Jeet makes at the paper in a year. I mean, no kidding, she would go jetting off to the East Coast or even Europe to take a lesson with the biggies, say a Hans, a Jürgen, a Reiner, a Katerina, somebody *major*) she'd come back, and guess what? She'd still ride like a piece of luggage. I loved it.

At a show I and just about everyone else in the club could whip her ninety percent of the time. I mean with fjord ponies, practically, those square ponies that look like shag rugs. I mean, that's how bad she was, even when she was mounted on those multithousand-dollar honeys of hers.

One time she showed training level against a woman who was now a really strong Olympic hopeful, Texas's own Melissa Song. Even now Melissa hardly ever shows, but this time, the first time I'd seen her, she was trying out a new and very young horse, the horse that is now expected to win us the gold. But anyway, the point is, Melissa's score had been seventy-five and Nika's had been forty-two. That probably means nothing to you, but in the dressage biz, anything under fifty means you should probably be bowling instead of riding and anything sixty or above means break out the champagne. A seventy-five is a practically unheard of score and a forty-two is ignominy. Talk about being beaten senseless!

God, I still remember that day. Nika was resplendent, her spurs and her stirrups and the bit in her horse's mouth gleaming in the sunlight. Right up until the very last minute Manuel was polishing her boots while Nika patted her coif, which was smoothed back impeccably into an invisible net.

Off in the corner was Melissa, an actual Indian—Cherokee, I think. She wore white sweat pants instead of breeches and the grass stains on her knee had smudged into a neon green where she'd tried and failed to wipe them off. Her left boot had a torn seam and you could see her red sock through it.

Her horse was beautiful, but shaggy, his winter coat only partially gone. His mane had not been pulled but cut instead with scissors, the equivalent of a human haircut done with a cereal bowl.

We all looked askance at this poor girl, whom none of us knew. We were all thinking that here, at last, was someone even Nika could beat.

Ha!

Nika entered the arena the way she always did, with everything—hands, legs, torso even—jiggling. She yanked the horse into a halt and—hey, you get the picture. The entire test went this way.

Melissa, on the other hand, was the picture of grace. No kidding, from the minute she gathered up her reins, she was transformed. All of the stuff about her and her horse's appearance proved to be superficial as she glided through the best test I've ever witnessed. It was only training level, walk-trot-canter, but it was the first time for me that a training-level test had been as exhilarating as a classical ballet. You don't believe me? Let me tell you what happened when she was through. The scribe—the person who sits next to the judge to record the comments that the judge makes during the test—stood up and applauded.

And after leaving the arena, Melissa just disappeared. Didn't hang around to get her ribbon or her trophy or even the scored test sheet. It was like, Who was that masked man?

Anyway, that was the only time I ever saw Melissa Song in person and that was the first time I ever saw Nika in the throes of purple-faced—as opposed to something quieter and more deadly—wrath. Nika was waving the American Horse Shows Association rule book and trying to get Melissa disqualified because she'd been wearing sweats instead of bona fide breeches.

The judge professed—and it was probably the truth—not to have noticed. Melissa's to-die-for score of seventy-five stood.

And dumbo Nika blamed the loss on her horse, selling him before she even left the show grounds for something like twenty thou—maybe half of what she'd paid. Of course, by the time Nika was finished with a horse, he was always worth far less than what she'd paid. Or is that snide?

Ah, but snide or not, as a result of this memory, the *other* part of what had been plaguing me about Nika's photo in the FEI duds fell into place: this was *not* one of Nika's horses in the picture.

I couldn't wait to call Lola to tell her what I'd figured

out. Except that when I told Lola everything that I've told you, she groaned and said, "Hey, I don't think I'd go around talking about beating Nika senseless and to-die-for scores. Not right now. Know what I mean?"

That kind of brought me back to the reality of the thing. I mean, here was this woman, someone I *knew*, and she was finito, dead, murdered. I felt a little spooked about being home alone. "Can I come over?" I said.

"Since when do you have to ask?"

And I was on my way.

Lo lives on the farm that adjoins our place, and if you cut through the woods, it's a literal hop, skip, and jump. If you go by roads, it's a bit more complex. Lo's house is ancient, a former stagecoach stop or something and there's a Texas historical plaque on the porch by the door. The spread itself is small by overall Texas standards—one hundred and thirty acres—but big by Austin standards. Jeet says Lo is sitting on a gold mine.

Lola and I had never talked about the place or the land; I mean the dollar value or whatever. I knew her father had left it to her. I don't think she ever even considered selling it.

And anyway, it was just as well. The bottom had fallen out of the Texas economy, like everything was for sale and nobody was buying.

All of this meant that I had a dandy place to ride, since our own Primrose Farm is pretty tiny. It also meant that Lo and I have spent countless hours in what is a necessary offshoot of dressage: arena maintenance. And I'm not talking a big fancy arena like the indoor at Cliffside, with mirrors along all of the walls and a sprinkler system overhead in case things get dusty. I'm talking yardage out in the middle of a big open field

Yardage that Lola and I combed for rocks and dragged for levelness and all but knelt in front of the way Muslims do their temples (if it's Muslims who do that).

"We ought to find out more about that picture," I began even as I entered.

"What picture?" She was filling a kettle, probably for tea.

"God, Lola, how could you forget?" I reminded her about the top hat and the fancy duds. Lola, in response, put the kettle down and pretended to be throwing up.

"Really," I said. "You ought to see it."

"Right, like I'll die unless."

"Look, we don't have to obsess about it. We'll just go one time, to the TV station, and we'll ask about it."

"We?"

I looked as wistful as I could. "We owe it to Nika," I said.

"Oh, bull," Lola countered. "You just want to snoop around. You want to know about that horse and about those clothes, and you don't care what you have to go through to find out about them, either. You're a total and hopeless gossip monger."

This could have led to an am-not/are-too exchange, but I was mature enough about it to let the comment slide.

"I *do* want to know what she was doing in that outfit," I admitted. "I mean *her* of all people. And forget how she was dressed. Who would ever even let her sit on an FEI horse?"

"It didn't have to be an FEI horse," Lola said. "It could have been a horse that was stuffed, for that matter." We both laughed at that. Because in dressage, especially, you don't let just anybody up on your horse. Oh, friends, maybe, when their training methods and

philosophy and level of skill are about the same as your
own. The standard joke is that you'd let someone sleep
with your husband before you'd let her ride your horse.
"How did it look?" she went on.

"How did what look?"

"The *horse*."

"Elegant. No kidding, star quality. Presence, arro-
gance, the whole enchilada."

"Did he look happy?"

"Happy? You mean ears pricked forward, soft eyes,
that kind of thing?"

She nodded yes, yes.

"Yeah. He looked happy."

"Well, see," she said. "It probably was a stuffed
horse."

"Oh, what the hell, Lola. It's just a ride to the TV
station, for God's sake."

"What about Jeet?" she asked. "What does he say
about going?"

"I don't know, I haven't mentioned it."

"Oh, great. The man doesn't hate me enough."

But actually, Lola exaggerates. Jeet is suspicious of
Lola, that's all. He's suspicious because, like Jeet and
me, she's in her thirties, only *she's* single and *she* dates.
He thinks she's too old to be single and he thinks she's
too old to be dating. And he also thinks that Lola is a
bad influence on me. Not that I'm going to date or anything, but that, in Lola's clutches, I'm going to hear
intimate details about other men.

This might not be true. Jeet has never said so. But
it's what I think, based on how edgy he gets if I rib
Lola about someone she's seeing. He gets very, I don't
know, *priggish*. His attitude definitely loosened up back
when Lo had announced that she was getting married
to Cody, which of course never happened.

"Come on, Lola," I said now.

She let a whistle of air rush out between her teeth. This meant she was weakening. "I still have two of my guys to ride," she told me.

"I'll ride one of them."

"Okay."

Lola thinks of dressage as "an old-lady sport." Combined training—dressage plus jumping—is her thing. The number of horses that she has fluctuates, but usually she runs about four. That's three more than I have—and she spends all day every day keeping them in shape. It's the way Lola makes her living: buying, rehabilitating, campaigning, reselling. In my case, it's all for love. Still, I don't guess, unless you ride seriously yourself, that you realize there are people like Lola, or for that matter, me. But we're out there, droves of us. We're not world-class riders, by any means. But the sport—with its incessant demands on our pocketbooks and our time and our bodies and our psyches— has us totally by the tail.

I remember when Jeet found this out about me. We had known each other a couple of months, and he'd asked me to go on a citrus-tasting trip with him to the Rio Grande Valley. "Oh, great," I'd told him. "I have some friends down there."

Horse folks, of course.

Anyway, we were in their pool house, changing. I came out of the cubicle and found him staring at the wall, where my chums had a huge poster hung.

"Oh, my God," Jeet was saying, "I'm with a bunch of fanatics."

"Huh?" I asked.

"Fanatics," he repeated. "You people are crazy."

I looked at the poster, then back at him. "What are you talking about?" I asked.

"You don't even know," he said.

"Know what?"

What Jeet was staring at looked perfectly normal to me ("Exactly my point," he'd say), a map labeled *Horse Map of the World*. On it, the places where the different breeds had emerged had been marked with little horse's heads. Like Hanover in Germany, and Nez Percé territory here, etc. Big deal.

All that week, at odd moments, I'd hear Jeet mutter, "Horse Map of the World." Sometimes he'd shake his head, as if it were something sad. He eventually pulled out of this, and now, I daresay, he wouldn't bat an eye at an artifact like that. But it did sort of indicate to me how odd the world at large finds the horse person's obsession.

"If we go to the television station," Lola shouted as we galloped up a long, grassy slope, "will you stop?" She was over the top and had started down the other side, not slowing her pace at all.

I pushed my horse to keep up with her. If I hadn't been talking, I probably would have been scared. "Stop what?" I yelled.

She pulled up enough for me to come alongside. "You know very well what." She looked over at me. "Snooping."

"You aren't curious?"

"I think the police should handle it."

"They probably are."

"Or Ron."

"Ron's probably the one who—" I stopped talking, horrified by what I'd almost said about Nika's husband. What was my problem? Why was I thinking that? Could it be that with Nika gone, the considerable drain she'd been making on Ron's income would be, too? I mean, what did Nika spend on horses anyway? Except that even I knew that this whole line of thinking was born of nothing more than envy. I mean, sure, I'd like it if I could say, "Jeet, that five-thousand-dollar Hermes saddle in the Miller's catalog . . ." and he would say, "Done!" and whip out his checkbook. Which, by the way, is how the dressage rumor mill said things were in the Ballinger household. (As some wag once put it, "If the first question you ask when you meet a new couple isn't 'Is it his money or her money?' you aren't truly adult.")

These philosophical goings-on were interrupted by Lola. "I'm going to jump that," she said, gesturing toward a fallen log with a lot of cactus around it. "You coming?"

"You first," I called, stopping my horse even though I knew that following close behind her was the better, safer way. An involuntary response. I mean, so far I'd rejoiced that we hadn't gone near any of the real jumps Lo had built. Now here was an impromptu. It wasn't high, but the cactus made it look forbidding—kind of like the scene in that old movie *The List of Adrian Messenger*, where the fox hunt keeps getting closer and closer to this fence with some really nasty farm equipment parked on the landing side.

I watched as Lola slowed her pace a bit and headed toward the jump.

But it wasn't like the movie at all. In fact, Lola's horse just sailed over the jump, making it look just as easy as could be. Lola was waiting for me now. "Any day you're ready," she hollered.

The jump was as low as they come, and it seemed stupid, even while I was feeling my fear, to be afraid. But the fact is, I hadn't galloped cross-country, much less jumped, since my dreadful fall three years earlier. And Lola knew it.

My horse began to get a little dancy—as if he were impatient with me, too.

"All right," I said, leaning forward and gathering my reins. I grabbed two fistfuls of mane as well.

But Lola's horses—by the time they went out like this—were dreamboats. They liked to jump, every one of them. All you had to do was aim.

I aimed. And the horse just carried me, steady as can be, up and over and beyond. Except that truth be told, I'd *still* been terrified, my every nerve fiber shrieking No! No! No! each step of the way. I tried to bluff it out, though. I even laughed when I pulled the horse up. "What a packer he is," I said, patting him.

But Lola, I think, could tell. A brief expression— pity?—crossed her face. And then, "Okay," she decided. "The television station and that's all. Let's cool these guys out."

We kicked our stirrups loose, let our legs dangle, and rode in on a loose rein, the horses blowing contentedly and quickening their walk as they realized they were headed home.

We stopped to let them reach down to sip water out of the tank. A tank is what they call a pond down here. You can imagine how peaceful and pastoral this was, the water rippling lightly in the breeze, the thin-leafed mesquite branches swaying to and fro, the horses with their mouths immersed, drinking silently.

Suddenly, both at once, they tensed and their heads came up really high, like giraffes'. They were staring, and by now we were, too, at two men in city clothes— white shirts and ties—walking toward us.

The men came with their wallets outstretched, badges glinting in the sun. They were wary of the horses, and the animals responded in kind. While Lo and I both shortened our reins and closed our legs on the horses' sides to calm them down, the men stopped, and one of them—the taller of the two—asked me if I was Lola Albright.

I moved my head in Lo's direction. It felt like a betrayal, somehow. Both men now advanced upon her. I saw her face sort of settle into a meeting-hostile-strangers mode: eyes narrow, brows slightly raised, smile less than real. Her cheeks burned red.

I guess I should have mentioned how gorgeous Lola is. About six inches taller than I am, and maybe twenty-five pounds lighter, too. And if that's not enough, she's got a mass of coal-black hair that kinks and curls and tumbles all around.

"Miz Albright, we'd like to have a word with you."

"In private," the taller one said.

Men are usually a little disconcerted in her presence, but not this time.

Lola dismounted immediately. She walked toward me and handed me her reins. "You mind?" she said. Her features softened as she spoke to me.

I shook my head no.

Then she led the two men back toward the house while I made my way to the stable yard.

I was in the wash rack hosing down horse number two when Lola came out with the men. She still wore her breeches, but had substituted tennies for her boots. She had her huge black musette bag with her.

She looked vulnerable and defiant all at once. The defiance came from the way she tossed and then lifted her head. But then, she was also kind of biting her lower lip. She'd plopped a pair of wraparound shades on and her favorite gimme cap, the one with *Stable Boy* emblazoned on the front and steaming horse apples embroidered on the sides. I stepped out where I knew that she could see me, if she looked.

But she didn't look. She slid into the back of the unmarked car as if she were an actress—a slightly worried actress—being whisked to a premiere.

I watched the car move off and felt as if I'd let her down. Like, I should have been chasing the car, yelling at the police, telling the police that they were making a huge mistake.

I mean, they were, weren't they? Unless somebody had it in for Lola, maybe playing up the Cody thing. Except that that was ridiculous. It wasn't as though Lola had been carrying a torch. I'd seen her with Nika at shows, and while she didn't seek out Nika's company, she was civil enough when they met.

Don't get me wrong; I'm no dummy. I know full well that in human relations duplicity is often the name of the game. Or hypocrisy at least. But I also know that Lola wasn't that way. If she'd hated Nika, I, at least, would have known about it.

I went into the house and tried to call Jeet. No luck. I tried to call Vince with the same result. Then I poured a bunch of dry food out for Lola's cats. Then I thought it's better not to talk about the police taking Lo, at least not until the thing blows over. Because if Jeet didn't like Lola before, this would do it, for sure.

No matter how long Lo was gone, the horses, I realized, would be fine. Lo had a University of Texas student, Suzie, who came every day to grain, clean stalls, whatever. Still, they'd have to be worked, wouldn't they? I made a plan to exercise them on the longe line every day, or ask Suzie to, at least. The longe is a line several meters long. The horse at the end of it moves around the trainer in a circle. Horses can stay in shape forever that way.

Then I caught myself. I was jumping to conclusions. Suppose the police only wanted to ask Lola a couple of questions? I mean, here I was, leaping to the worst possible conclusion (as, I confess, is often my wont).

Still, if they were only questioning her, they'd have done it here, wouldn't they? This had to be more serious than that.

I went into the bathroom and looked for Lola's toothbrush. It was there. I almost breathed a sigh of relief. Then I thought that maybe she'd been too upset to think of it, and I was off and worrying again.

I went back into the main part of the house, which still smelled like cinnamon from Lola's tea. I walked around, letting my hands rest on some of Lola's things. Her dad's old green leather chair. Her mom's paisley shawl. A huge gnarled clay-potted geranium. A tangle of philodendron spilling out of a huge Maxwell House coffee can. A tarnished silver challenge trophy she'd won, now stuffed with papers, maps, and old dressage tests.

These cops were bozos, I thought. Didn't they realize that murderers didn't live in comfortable old houses that looked this way and smelled this way and felt this way, warm and easy?

I began looking through the stuff in the trophy, absentmindedly, of course. A lot of the papers were bills. And a lot of the bills were marked *Overdue, Final Notice*, that kind of thing.

But so what? Lola just hadn't gotten around to them. Some people were just that way. It made Lola even more lovable somehow.

CHAPTER 2

Though my sense of adventure had been muted by what had just taken place, I decided to go to the television station, anyway. It would give me something to do. Something constructive. Something that might just help my friend.

Not surprisingly, the station turned out to be in one of those industrial parks on the edges of Austin proper. You know the kind I mean, the kind where there are storage lockers and places where you can have speakers and a CD player put inside your car.

I was kind of glad about this because it's very hard to find a place downtown that's long enough to enable me to park my truck legally.

I call it the Mother Ship, because it's a long-bed super-cab '79 Dodge. In other words, *humongously big*. Which is to say that eventually I can get into a parking spot, but after all the back and forth with the steering wheel and all the gear grinding, my deodorant has been overpowered and I'm drenched with sweat—hair, skin, clothes, everything—and exhausted besides. Plus I'm in a bad mood. Attractive, right?

At any rate, in the industrial park I am able to choose from several huge spaces. I cruise into two of them. Thus I am able to smile brightly at the sleek and impeccably groomed receptionist behind the high-tech chrome-and-black Formica pod of a desk.

But she doesn't smile back. Nor is her message one of encouragement. "Graphics is a nightmare," she says, widening her eyes, so that they looked like targets. "You'll never find that picture now."

"What do you mean *now*?" By my count, it had been less than twenty-four hours since they'd run it.

"They used it yesterday, Sunday, so it's been here overnight. With the weekend crew. Believe me, it will never be seen again."

I consider grabbing her white silk lapels and yanking her up from her desk. "Find it or else," I'd say, and then she'd scurry off, either to get it or to bring back the security force. Instead, however, I lie. "That was my only copy," I say. "Nika Ballinger was"—I pause to swallow, and she interprets it as an attempt to fight back tears—"my sister."

The receptionist has pulled her chair back from the desk to look at me. Her eyes and mouth are pulled in toward her nose. She has one eyebrow now, like Frida Kahlo. "Oh . . . oh . . . please don't . . ."

I see that I'm getting to her. "My *only* sister," I say. I'm imagining now how Lola would react to this performance. "My only sister"—sniff—"who is dead."

The receptionist is on her feet. She is pushing a box of Kleenex across the surface of the pod. She is making strange little noises, probably of comfort, and she is backing away toward a door that is camouflaged to look like the walls.

I am alone with my grief. I apply lip gloss.

When she handed me the manila envelope with *Graphics* stamped across the front, it was all I could do to stay in character. "Thank you *so* much." I looked deeply into her eyes.

"You have my sympathy," she said. "My deepest sympathy." Her mouth began to twitch and guilt started edging its way into my consciousness. I forced myself to think of all the *Rockford Files* reruns I'd watched. Heck. Rockford never felt guilty, and he was a decent guy. So I nodded as if I and the woman were somehow solemnly bonded and I winked at my own reflection on the way out. This was easy. Maybe I should become a PI.

I drove straight to a seemingly customerless juice stand. I propped the photo up on the dash while I studied it. It was Nika, for sure. And also for sure, the duds were the real thing, FEI garb. And the horse was ultra-luxe and not one that I'd ever seen before.

People who don't know horses think that other than color, they look pretty much alike. And some poll or other that one of the horse magazines took said that even horse owners can't remember specifics about their own mounts, like which leg is white and how far up, for instance.

At the same time, though, horse people can, by some weird gestalt, separate a horse they know from a thousand others marked exactly alike.

It's little things, like with people, a way of cocking the head, or carrying the rump, or a particular light in the eyes. Which is to say, I knew in my *cojones*—or would have if I'd had *cojones*—that this wasn't a local horse, wasn't even a horse that Nika had owned in the past.

Lord knows, Lola and I had been subjected to Nika's never-ending march of photos and videotapes. Once we'd even watched a video of a sonogram of one of her horses tumbling it its dam's womb, I swear. Nika, like a lot of other horse people, wanted a record of her every show, her every ride. In her case, *America's Funniest Home Videos* might have been interested, too.

But to return to the matter at hand, good as my horse memory is, it wasn't able to connect the horse in the photograph with any that I'd ever seen or known. Maybe Lo was right and it was a stuffed horse after all.

It had been nearly three hours since Lo had been arrested. Time enough, wouldn't you say, for the police to allow me to visit her. I'd show her the photo and maybe she could come up with who the horse was. And I'd get to tell her, too, that no matter what, I'd be there. Robin Vaughan was on the case, playing out her hunch.

Hunch? you say. Well, in a way it was. I mean, in dream analysis they always tell you to examine the most irrational part of the dream. The secret meaning, they say, is there. I ask you, why wouldn't this translate to a murder? Ergo, my technique.

I had to park illegally at the Austin PD, because there were only spaces for ordinary cars. You have to wonder why since nearly everyone in Texas drives a truck. Still, I couldn't imagine that they'd give me a ticket in front of the police station, of all places. They'd figure it was some kind of emergency, wouldn't you think? Because why else would I have parked there?

I sashayed inside. I asked for Homicide. Yet another receptionist—this one a young cop in uniform—asked me if I was reporting one.

"No," I said, clipping my words Joe Friday style. "Here to see my friend. Best friend. Lola Albright. She's a suspect. The Nika Ballinger case."

He relayed this to someone by phone. And then he

turned to me, and as he did I saw Vince out of the corner of my eye.

It's amazing how reflex takes over. Because before Vince could even glance in my direction, I ducked down—I mean fell like a stone—and started moving in a sort of bent-over scoot around the big desk, to the far side. It wasn't that I wouldn't own up to having been at the police station, understand. I mean, I would eventually. It was just that the time wasn't *now*, because, if you'll recall, I had decided not to let Jeet know about Lola's predicament. And believe me, if Vince knew, Jeet would know, too.

But meanwhile, the receptionist cop was threatening to spoil everything, peering down over the desk at me and saying, "Ma'am? Ma'am?" I gave him the shoosh sign and tried to look fervent and beseeching, but he kept right on.

And worse, he spoke to me at maybe three times the decibel level he'd have otherwise used. "You can't see Lola Albright," he shouted, and I held my breath, wondering if Vince had heard it, too.

Apparently not. I heard the door to the street whoosh shut and was able to stand up.

"You can't see Lola Albright because"—the young cop was bellowing the way you do to explain to old people, dumb people, foreign people—"she, Lola Albright—"

And then it hit me: My truck! Vince was bound to see it parked out there! I screamed, "Oh, no!" and bolted for the door. I could always beg Vince not to tell Jeet right away, couldn't I?

The cop fell silent. He was, I presume, regarding me with openmouthed astonishment. I didn't want him to think I was nuts. So I yelled back over my shoulder, "Oh, right, I know, I can't see her. Of course I can't see her. I get it.'' I wanted to add that I'd read *The Gulag Archipelago*, but I was sure that the information would be lost on him.

And guess. I did get a ticket. I pocketed it the way folks usually do, with an air of insouciance. Ticket, hey, no problem. But the good news was, Vince was nowhere to be seen. Unless . . . nah. He'd have waited to confront me.

I was new to the snooping business. I was learning by doing. So I could expect to be slow. By which I mean that it finally dawned on me, why not *use* Vince, use his police connections to find out what was going on? Vince, because of his job, probably had some hardcore data. Me, I had never even, until now, been inside a genuine police station before.

So now I was running up the street, *looking* for the man who, moments earlier, I'd made a total fool of myself trying to avoid. And because I *was* looking, he had—*poof!*—disappeared. I went through the whole parking lot, looking for one of the newspaper's staff cars, and it was no go.

Which I would have been able to live with, I guess, if it weren't for the fact that when I got back to my truck, there was yet *another* ticket on the windshield.

So great. Now I was going to have to go to court and fight, protest for all of the super-cab long-bed truck drivers in and around Austin.

I was sucking on a frozen yogurt (butterscotch, sugar free, fat free) while I got my wits together and decided what was next. As before, I propped the photo of Nika up and communed with it, as if there were something it might tell me. I could almost hear Nika braying, enjoying the fact that Lola was languishing in jail because of her.

* * *

Lo's place was my next stop, just to make sure that Suzie was there and that she wasn't planning to make a field trip to Belize or the Yucatán or some such. She was an art major, primitive stuff, with a Latin American specialty.

This fit right in with dressage. Nearly everybody in it had a degree or two or three, and still, their all-consuming interest was the sport. All their degrees did, usually, was provide the wherewithal to indulge this extravagant passion. So the few men and the multitude of women in dressage were surgeons and stockbrokers and heiresses and engineers and lawyers and entrepreneurs. Nika herself had a degree in something, classical archaeology, I think she once said. Not that she ever used it.

Me? I'd been in phys. ed. I can still remember Jeet sputtering about that, as if it were the absolute pits as majors go. Until of course I'd found out *his* major: home ec. But anyway, all that's beside the point, because what I'm talking about is that dressage attracts a lot of highly intelligent people. Of course this also means that everyone is adept at insult and also as opinionated as can be.

Witness Suzie, who, despite her fresh, good looks (blond hair, pixie cut, a sprinkling of freckles), greeted me with a chorus of "Ding-dong the Witch Is Dead." Suzie used to work for Nika at Cliffside.

Still, I didn't laugh. Especially not with Lo's neck in the noose.

"Oh, come on, Robin," Suzie persisted. "Everyone hated Nika's flaming, stinking guts."

"Did you?"

"Naturally." I wondered what Nika had done to Suz, but while I was wondering she told me. Suz had finally found a talented horse that didn't cost the moon, and Nika bought the animal out from under her. "And then she ruined him, pounded him into the ground,'' Suzie finished.

"Who was it?'' I asked. "Which horse?''

Suzie looked vague. "No one you know,'' she said, eyes looking over my shoulder.

It wasn't important, so I went on. "So did you snuff her?'' I asked. I think I was expecting to shock her with my use of this term.

But she giggled. "I wish.''

This was rubbing me the wrong way. I mean, I didn't like Nika either, but I don't think I would have acted quite so cavalier. On the other hand, maybe it was generational. Maybe Suzie was typical of the youth of today, right out of *Less Than Zero*.

The youth of today. Did I say that? Did saying that move me into a new category, as in the middle-aged of today? Oh, God. I went on with my interrogation.

"Suzie,'' I said, taking the photograph of Nika out for her inspection, "Have you ever seen this horse?''

"Oh, gross,'' Suzie said, when she saw it was Nika. "Her? Riding FEI?''

I tried again. "Have you ever seen this horse?''

"Yeah,'' she said slowly. "Yeah, but I don't know where. Recently, though.'' She closed her eyes and clapped a hand over them the way a clairvoyant might. "No, no. I can't remember.'' She opened her eyes and handed the photo back to me. "I just can't believe her in those clothes,'' she said. "And she was skinny then, too.''

"Did you ever see her dressed that way?''

"Get real.''

"No, really, think about it. Did you ever see clothes like that hanging up somewhere? Like in her closet.''

"Closet, right. Like she'd let a grunt of hers look inside one of her closets.''

A light went on in my brain. "What about me? I could look. You know what Ron is like. Do you think he'd let me?"

A slight blush fell across her face. "Do what?" she asked. "Go through Nika's closet?"

"Yeah."

"Jeez, I don't know. And when would you do it, anyhow?"

"What do you mean, when?"

"Like the funeral's tomorrow," she said. "So when?"

"Tomorrow?" Wasn't that uncommonly soon? I mean, wasn't there some kind of waiting period or something?

Suzie must have read my mind. "Tomorrow is like three days, okay?" Then she lowered her voice confidentially. "What I heard is, they autopsied her right after they pulled the plug. So I guess Ron figured why wait around? So anyway, when?"

Why wait around indeed. I wondered if Jeet would ditch me that quickly. On the other hand, it did seem ghoulish to have an embalmed body all lipsticked and rouged and lying in state for everyone to go see. "When what?" I asked.

"Nika's closet. If you ask to go through it right after the funeral, wouldn't it be kind of impolite?"

Impolite, right. But who was I to be thinking morally superior thoughts? Because even as I was thinking how ice cold Suzie was about all of this, a little voice was advising me when to plunder Nika's things. *During the funeral,* the voice was saying, *that's when. During.*

CHAPTER 3

"I don't know, I just feel sick," I told Jeet. Needless to add, after fruitlessly searching for Vince, I hadn't needed to mention anything about Lola's plight. And, I'm relieved to report, neither had Jeet. I mean, if he even suspected that Lola was in a jam, he'd never buy this sick thing. I know they have no apparent connection, but trust me: Jeet would know. As it stood, I had a real chance of pulling this off, which meant I—and Lola, too—would be home free.

Marriage is tough, no question.

Jeet clapped his hand on my forehead. "Hmmm," he said.

"Hmmm what?"

He was doctorly, which meant that he didn't bother to answer that. "Do you have a headache?" he asked.

"A little bit."

"Sore throat?"

"No."

"Aches? Pains?"

I guess I should have thought my symptoms out ahead of time. Too late now. "Well, kind of . . ." And then I shifted my weight and gave a little whimper. "I do feel kind of nauseous."

Jeet's brow twitched. "Nauseated," he corrected.

"You feel nauseated." Despite our disparate majors, it had been an honors English class where we'd met.

"Whatever." I pulled the covers up over my chin and tried to look waiflike.

"Good," Jeet said, bounding toward the bathroom.

"Good?"

"I can deal with nauseated," he shouted out.

I could hear the *plop plop fizz fizz*. "I still don't think I can go to the funeral, though." I held my breath and waited.

"Of course you can't go," he said.

I breathed.

Then he emerged from the bathroom to thrust the concoction, all hiss and foam, in front of my face. "Now drink."

And, alas, he folded his arms and watched me do it.

If you don't think that was so bad, wait until you hear the next part. Because, after some minor pillow fluffing and a brief tuck-in, he went downstairs.

Within minutes I could hear the Cuisinart doing its stuff. This was followed by the luscious smell of maple and nuts of some kind. Then there was a sizzle, the kind that meant that butter had gone into the pan. I was on the verge of leaping up from my bed like someone who'd been miraculously cured. "I can walk! I can see! I can smell!" I would shout as I made my way toward the kitchen.

But of course I couldn't do it, because it would mean that I was throwing Lola to the wolves. So I held my nose and tried to concentrate on how I'd look if I lost ten pounds. If I lost ten pounds and bought a pair of those pouchy breeches, the kind Faye Dunaway wore in *Chinatown*, the kind that make even me look as though I have a waist. And then—I mean, this was fantasy, so why not—if I had a massive Holsteiner stallion, so massive that even if I *gained* ten pounds, I'd look absolutely tiny on his back.

By then Jeet was back, humming and tying his tie. He looked handsome and clean. He is both, of course. A little on the rumpled side, I guess you'd be forced to say. You know, a shock of poker-straight hair falling straight across his brow much of the time; tie, when he's wearing one, a tad askew.

"What did you have to eat?" I asked, pointing at a powdery something on his lapel.

He drew his head to the side, as if trying to see the place I meant. "You don't want to hear about it, hon. It'll just make you throw up."

"No, really. Tell me." I pointed to indicate that the place on his coat was higher.

He stood there brushing with the flat of his hand. "Belgian waffles. Maple-nut butter. A dusting of—"

"All right, you can stop." I meant the spot on his coat was gone, but he thought I was talking about the menu.

"Just get some rest." Jeet's lips against my forehead. My arms around his neck. Then Jeet's lips for real. He always smells so spicy and good. He smiled at me. "I'll give Ron your sympathy, okay?"

My weak nod. And then my valiant and hopeful, "Leave the dishes. I'll clean up."

When he'd driven away, I dived down the stairs and stumbled into the kitchen. I'd take anything, any crumb, any bit of sauce. But Jeet, being Jeet, had already tidied up. Dishes rinsed and in the dishwasher. Remnants of waffle and the sauce in the trash. And not just in the inside trash, either, but outside in the garage. I stared at the bit of waffle, that golden sticky sauce that dappled its surface.

Minutes later, without even trying to call the police station again, I leaped into the truck and careened toward Cliffside by way of the drive-through at McDonald's.

By the time I got to the farm, Ron was long gone. I parked discreetly on the road. And then I made my way up the cliff that gave the place its name.

I picked a not-so-steep part, of course. Then I grabbed whatever there was to grab and thus propelled myself along. I probably could have taken the driveway, but no self-respecting detective in the movies or on TV would have done that. Fortunately, I was wearing my all-purpose, all-size, indestructible army-green poplin shift. If anybody spotted me, I figured, I could always stand still with my arms straight out and pretend to be a tent someone had pitched. Meanwhile, I couldn't help wishing that there was *something*, anything, growing in Texas that wasn't prickly or spiked or thorny.

I was also very aware, more aware than I would have liked to be, of the rattlesnake, tarantula, scorpion, and fire-ant populations. About the only thing in my favor was the fact that the killer bees were still dawdling farther to the south of the state. I *hate* these things about Texas.

And while we're on the subject, you may as well know that I do not participate in the Texas-My-Texas allegiance so prevalent here. I do not own a Texas shaped belt buckle, nor do I serve Texas-shaped chicken-fried steaks or pasta formed in the shape of the state. Do you think I'm kidding? Probably one out of five houses with stepping-stones has them cast in The Shape. No joke.

If you don't think that's weird, let me ask you, have you ever seen *anything* shaped like New Jersey? Or West Virginia? Or Utah?

(Jeet once went to a crabfest on Maryland's Eastern Shore. There, he said, there are a lot of people, mostly old ladies, obsessed with the profile of ducks. He saw ducks stamped on T-shirts and purses, duck artifacts in people's homes. But that's the only other thing I've heard that's remotely similar to the Texas thing. And anyway, ducks make a kind of sense.)

When I'd completed all of this musing, I was underneath one of the rear decks. When I'd shinnied onto it and peered through the French doors, I thought it was a child's room. Except that Nika and Ron didn't have any children, any that I knew about, at any rate.

I reached for the knob to try the doors and had a momentary twinge of conscience.

This was serious. This was real. If I cranked this knob, I'd be breaking and entering.

I thought of Lola. I thought of the way she'd stepped into that unmarked car. I thought of Nika. Of the way that her lips formed into a nasty little pinch whenever she saw anyone she'd one-upped.

I turned the knob and the door swung open.

Since it was unlocked, I figured that I wasn't breaking after all. I was merely entering. And I did dust myself off and even wipe my feet as I did.

I sort of ignored the room and went off down the hall in search of the master suite.

I listened first, of course. Nothing but a steady hum, like the AC or the fridge. This made the house sound even emptier.

Oh God. It's odd how you can do something (like sleuth around) and forget *why* you're doing it. At the same time I fought against remembering. Against thinking that the sound was what Nika was hearing in her coffin, that the place was one giant coffin, with the lid about to close.

I had to actually fold my arms around myself and say, "Shhh, shhh," a couple of times to go on with why I was here. And eventually it worked.

I found what had to be a guest room, small, with empty closets. Another that apparently saw similar use. And one that maybe belonged to Ron alone, all brown and tweedy with men's toiletries and hunting magazines. One that contained Nautilus equipment and free weights. Another that was set up as a sitting room, though I couldn't tell why.

I soon deduced that the room I'd come into was obviously the one that was Nika's, so I made my way back there.

The decor there was so frothy, so all wrong. In fact, it looked rather like the inside of a huge bonbon, sort of silvery pink, with everything—bed, canopy, lampshades, the works—all poufy and silky and lacy.

There were stuffed animals all over the bed, a white unicorn and a teddy bear (also white), and a flop-eared bunny. Unless she used them to practice disembowelment or something, this was not the way I would have pictured Nika's lair.

Deep in my heart I thought it would be dungeonlike, with scarlet light bulbs and bordello-red walls. There'd be handcuffs and chains and her worn-out dressage whips or something, know what I mean?

Instead, here I was in Wonderland. I mean, even the rug in the room was so thick it was like walking on marshmallows. Pink ones.

Still, I didn't have a clue about where I ought to begin. Unless it was the closets, where her riding clothes might be.

Closet number one: wrong. This one was filled with formals and furs. Formals, all right, but how many times can you wear fur down here in Texas? If you'd *want* to wear fur, that is.

Closet number two: wrong. This was shoes and boots. Lots of shoes and boots. Everything from Mary Janes and actual saddle shoes to five-inch stilettos.

I took out one of the saddle shoes and wondered at it. Again, I thought that maybe the Ballingers had had a child. A child who had died. Or a child who was locked in another part of the house, the wine cellar, maybe. But when I measured the shoe against one of Nika's riding boots, I saw that both were the exact same size.

Hmmm.

I began routing through one of the drawers, even though I knew I wasn't going to find the FEI clothes there. Sure enough, there was Nika's underwear. Or some of it. Not push-up bras and silky little bikini panties, but childlike undershirts—I mean, really, even one with little blue teddy bears printed on it—and sensible white cotton briefs.

Strange lady, I thought. I mean, I knew about all her surgical attempts to remain youthful. This, I supposed, was an offshoot of that.

I shrugged and looked around, wondering what I ought to examine next.

I saw the door on the far side of the bathroom and made for it. Sure enough, it was Nika's dressing room. It looked sort of like a dry cleaner's shop, everything encased in bags on a revolving rack. I'd need a week to wade through all the clothing.

I found what seemed to be the riding-togs section. There, to accommodate Nika's yo-yo propensities, were breeches and shirts and jackets in every size. Really nice fabrics, too, with the kinds of textures only a lot of money can buy. I was salivating over a white linen show coat when I saw a big sort of yellowy-white jewelry box on the counter. It looked like ivory inlay. And it figured. In addition to having at so many of the fur-bearing critters, Nika had also had a hand in decimating the elephants.

I tapped at the box with my fingernail. It didn't seem to have a lock. That meant rifling it would be less illegal, right? And anyway, anything really valuable would be in a safe someplace, wouldn't it?

Under circumstances like these, you would wonder why this jewelry-box thing would bother me, wouldn't you? It was because jewelry was something that real crooks would actually steal. Clothes are something innocent. I can't imagine the police bursting into Nika's dressing room with pistols raised and saying, "Put down that Adolpho," or, "We've got the Donna Karan crook dead to rights." But some priceless brooch, that was something else again. Hence my hesitation.

Before I'd resolved this inner conflict, I heard a metallic squeaking. Like a door downstairs opening slowly, maybe?

I stood stock-still and listened. I felt my armpits getting damp. I tried to hold my breath, but after only seconds I felt hot and dizzy. I sucked air in, a big great gasp of it.

My mind eliminated Ron, because he'd have to be at his wife's funeral, right? So who? I tiptoed across the rug and I got as close to the open deadbolt door as I could.

I heard nothing. So I slithered, salamander style, along the hall until I reached a place where I could hear a faint swish-swish-swishing sound. It was unmistakably the whisper of the paper that's used to make the phone book. There was a pause, then the *click-beep* as buttons of a phone were being pressed.

Still on my belly, I moved back the way I'd come. Once I'd regained the boudoir, I found Nika's gilt-edged froufrou phone and made a grab for it. Static electricity zapped me, natch. And I was too late. All I heard was dial tone. I hung up, listening for the sound of the door again. I was salamandering yet again into the hall when it came.

I stood up, not even taking the time to unkink. I rushed downstairs and peered outside. But no one was visible from the entry and I didn't dare open the door. Then again, maybe it was the backdoor. I raced there— strike three.

My senses had been on high alert. Had the killer's been, too? Had the person maybe smelled that I was in the house and abandoned whatever it was he'd come to do? Or had he gone around back to surprise me?

These were not comforting thoughts. While entertaining them, I began to sweat. And then, because of the air-conditioning, I felt ice cold. At this rate, I wouldn't have to fake it. I really would be sick.

I rubbed my arms and started looking for the phone book, but there wasn't one anywhere in sight. It was as if I'd dreamed the whole thing up. Still, I lifted the receiver of the phone that the mystery person must have used and hit the redial button.

And bingo! The line was ringing on the other side. I felt triumphant. As though, in a scant second or two, I'd know who had really done it to Nika and why. And then I'd tell the police and I'd get them to release poor Lola. I'd be a hero. There'd be a ticker-tape parade. I'd go on all the talk shows, probably get a citation from the prez.

The ringing stopped. Then there was that hollow,

vaguely tinny sound that you get when someone's answering machine has taken the call.

Sure enough, a bright little voice began . . .

"Robin Vaughan here . . . well, not actually *here* but sort of here, either out in the barn or puttering around in the garden. So if you need to talk to Jeet or me . . ."

I lip-synched along with the recording and watched myself in the mirror, my head bobbing stupidly from side to side, my straight brown hair bouncing along with it. Gross. But I went through the entire dorky message this way.

I wondered: Why would a killer be calling me?

This meant, of course, that I would have to go to Nika's funeral after all. You see what I mean, don't you? Now I had to see who *wasn't* there.

CHAPTER 4

Do you remember Edie Adams's wonderful line about the wedding of one of LBJ's daughters? "Only the immediate country is invited," she said.

Well, Nika's funeral was like that, standing room only. Either *she* was very very popular or the fact that she'd departed this earthly realm was. I'd bet on the latter. In fact, Suzie had said that Nika's body wasn't being laid out on display in its coffin because the funeral director didn't want anyone to see the stake he'd had to place through her heart.

I myself had softened a bit toward the deceased. I don't know why, maybe because of those silly saddle shoes. There is something about seeing the secret side of a person.

For instance, I remember a piece a girl wrote once about her father, a minister. He'd just died and the paper had run it next to the official obit, which had read flat, like a résumé. The girl's piece cited all the little things about the man—the fact that at home he chewed Wrigley's Spearmint and washed with Palmolive Gold and that he'd always owned cats, the fact that he'd never even tried to eat a radish, and so on. The catalog, which at first seemed goofy, was eventually incredibly moving, because we could see the person that had been lost—the real person rather than the official one.

Thus, too, something about Nika—in a very wee voice, to be sure—had begun to speak to me. As if she'd worn those things, had that kind of a room, for a reason. I was even softening here, in the reason department. Now it wasn't to stay youthful, it was deeper than that. It was to regain her innocence, I thought now.

Still, when the minister began his eulogy, likening Veronika to a Thoroughbred and several times proclaiming, "She had heart, she had great heart," I chuckled as the people around me began to squirm. "Prove it," one man said. "Right," another seconded.

All this time, of course, I was in the balcony, figuring I'd be able to eliminate suspects that way. Thus far I'd crossed Willy Nelson and Ann Richards off the list. And it couldn't have been members of the city council in the house either, because they and the mayor, too, were all accounted for in what seemed to be a VIP section.

Did I mention that Ron is a major financier? Maybe financier is not right. Developer, I guess is what I mean. Buys land cheap, plops something on it, sells high. Environmental groups are constantly invoking his name. Said name was also prominently displayed in a *Texas Monthly* feature on the state's most influential men. Which is odd considering that to me he's always, even in juxtaposition to Nika, seemed like a gangster.

Anyway, I hadn't counted on this many people. I also hadn't counted on so many unrecognizable people. Partly, I realized, it was Street Clothes Syndrome. You see a bunch of people in riding clothes all the time and it's like having seen them nude because they all look pretty much alike. Then you see them in street clothes, and matters of taste come to the fore. There are those in fiesta attire, those who go for tailored. There are punks and there are preppies. You don't really know the folks you ride with until you've seen them in their civvies.

And then, too, there are the camouflage aspects of street clothes. For instance, at this very moment someone was probably looking at me and thinking: Surely that's not Thunder Thighs Vaughan.

So on top of the mob scene, I had this phenomenon to contend with. I decided right then and there to go downstairs and throw in the towel on the who-isn't-at-the-funeral aspect of my investigation.

Fortunately, the undertaker intervened. At least I thought he was the undertaker, all somber and damp-palmed. "Have you signed?" he asked a retreating couple, indicating, with a bow of his head, an open book, a registry of some sort, on a small, lighted podium.

The couple nodded. "On the way in," the woman said.

So all I had to do, really, was nab this little book and copy it. That way I could eliminate suspects like crazy. And I could put the book back when I was done, maybe on the floor so that those who'd missed it would surmise that it had fallen.

I was getting pretty good at this!

Except that so far, everything I'd done had been sub-rosa. Now I was faced with a situation that was more or less like shoplifting. I geared up for it, remembering the five-and-ten scene from *Breakfast at Tiffany's* and voilà! I was Audrey Hepburn in a cat mask.

I smiled at the undertaker and dawdled near the stand. He smiled at me. I rocked back on my heels, he rocked back on his. I stared. He fidgeted. I continued to stare. He fidgeted some more. And then he walked away.

* * *

So now I was in the twenty-four hour Kinko's, panting. Panting because I'd run here rather than drive. Needless to say, this meant that when I got here, there was a mammoth parking space right in front of the place, but never mind.

In addition, I had what seemed an ungodly long wait for a do-it-yourself machine. Although I'm not certain, I figure it must be term-paper time at UT. And the machine I finally got of course ran out of paper when I had only three more pages to go.

I began barreling back to the church, but about three or four blocks away I realized I was too late. I counted seven available parking spaces. Jeez, I could have parked Mother for free instead of paying actual money to put her in a lot. Except that the issue now wasn't parking, I reminded myself. It was the fact that the people inside the church had gone to the cemetery, for sure.

And I still had Ron's big black leather book.

Reading the pages I'd duplicated could wait, I thought, while I stopped yet again on the road that wound to Cliffside. What I had to do now was get this book back with the bereaved, where it belonged.

My plan was that I would smuggle the book into the house via the balcony I'd used before. Then I'd go downstairs and I'd just set it down where Ron wouldn't see it right away. When he found it, I reasoned, he would probably think some kind friend had brought it home. That or that he'd been too distraught to remember bringing it home himself. It was weak reasoning, I know, but under the circumstances, it would have to do.

Unless he wasn't distraught at all.

Ron, I thought. He's influential enough to have shifted suspicion from himself onto Lola.

Because it was Ron, you'll remember, I'd originally thought had done the deed. I'd practically said so back when Lo and I were riding, before her arrest. It wasn't that I had proof or anything. It was just that this is where my instinct first led me to turn.

Like shooting. Not that I've ever done any, but I'd seen an interview on television with a famous elk hunter. And he had said that when you hear a snap of twigs or a rustle of leaves in the forest and you turn toward it without thinking, you are inevitably aiming dead-on at your prey.

Of course, that conflicted with the theory I was working on, the business about investigating the most irrational part, but so what? An investigator has to be flexible.

I was raising myself onto the balcony—had one leg on it already, in fact—when I saw movement behind that set of bedroom doors. To be precise, I saw feet. High-heeled feet. Six of them. Moving around as if doing a dance. Then I looked up and saw the three young Mexican girls attached to those feet.

They didn't see me. They were too enthralled with Nika's formals. They were feeling them and giggling and holding them up against each other. Then they were holding them up against themselves, pretending to be wearing them and dancing.

I pulled my other leg up and got into what resembled a sitting pose. It was fascinating, watching this. They all seemed to be hearing the same music, too. A waltz.

Then, like an avenging angel, a beefy Mexican woman came into the room. She was wearing a stained white apron and carrying a wooden spoon. She was waving it, too.

All of the merriment stopped. The girls, with downcast eyes, dutifully hung the dresses back in Nika's closet. Then they picked up aprons from the floor where they'd been dropped. They tied the sashes behind their backs, then took hair nets from the apron pockets and restrained what collectively must have been thirty pounds of thick black hair. Finally, it was off with the slingbacks, on with the Keds. They filed sadly out of the room, presumably into the kitchen below.

Beefy, meanwhile, stepped across to the French doors. She opened them and stared down at me, spoon at the ready.

"Hi," I said, holding out my hand for a shake. "I'm her sister. Señora Ballinger's sister." Hey. It had worked before.

My hand hung there, naked and alone, suspended in midair while the woman appraised me. The woman continued to stare while I raked my memory for the Spanish word I needed. *Hermana*, I finally said, wondering if that was right.

"Ah," she replied.

To which I responded, *"Sí."* I figured that if the sister slant didn't work, I could always don a hair net and an apron and go downstairs and peel and dice with the rest of the catering crew. But fortunately, that wasn't necessary, because even as I was thinking it, Beefy said again, "Ah." Then she took my still-outstretched hand and helped me to my feet. Finally she believed me and started in with the excuses.

She had meant to put more pork in the ayocotes, *pero* gringos didn't seem to want more pork these days. She had meant to use whole peppercorns, *pero* she couldn't find her grinder. She had meant to marinate the chilies overnight, *pero* her mother called and she forgot all about it until morning. Finally she got to the *bueno*-bye stage and I was able to get downstairs to place the leather book on Ron's massive mahogany desk as planned, without incident.

I was able, too, to marvel at the room and its glass-eyed critters inhabiting every inch of wall. Killing animals is what Ron was evidently all about. It's nice to know that he and Nika had that bond. What a team, eh? He shot them, she wore them.

But this was no time to let my own morality intrude. After all, there were those who felt that riding horses was wrong. There were those, too, who thought horses should be diapered, if not clothed. So who was I to get huffy about the supply-and-demand arrangement Ron and Nika had?

And anyway, Nika wasn't wearing the *same* animals Ron had shot. I was letting myself get carried away. Still—I don't know if you know this, but there are a lot of exotic-game ranches here in Texas. They exist so that the locals can kill exotic game without actually having to travel to the animals' native land. Kind of like environmental home shopping.

But I digress, avoiding the sure and certain knowledge that the prudent thing for me to do at this point in my life would be to leave, go back to my sickbed, and wait for Jeet to make it home. What I ended up doing, however, was making another pass at Nika's dressing room.

This time I walked instead of crawled.

First I hit the jewelry box, which was empty of jewelry anyway. Nika seemed to use it as a kind of filing cabinet, with envelopes, mostly, laid flat in the shallow drawers.

Each had a different name written on the face, and most were folks I'd never heard of.

Then I came to one with my own name on the face.

It felt empty, but it wasn't. There was a single sheet of paper inside. A small sheet, off the kind of pad you'd set next to your phone. It was folded in half.

I opened it. My curiosity was so strong that I could feel the furrow in my brow. What I read made me reel.

Three words. It said:

> *Soiled Band-Aids*
> *Stocky*

I'm sure this means nothing to you. To me, however, it totally expunged even the tiniest little twinge of sympathy for Nika off the face of the planet.

Once—about three years ago—I lost twelve pounds in a single week. It was right after my mother had visited. She had gotten off the plane, hugged me, and then arm's-lengthed me. "Robin, you're so stocky!" she'd said.

Plump I could have handled. Stocky, though, made me feel as though I were built like a Jeep. Stocky made me feel as though hair were kinking on my legs and under my arms and even along my back. If there's anything I don't want to be, it's *stocky*.

And soiled Band-Aids, I mean *that* was just the pits. I don't know how Nika dug up that one, because I couldn't remember who I'd ever told. I mean, soiled Band-Aids don't exactly come up in day-to-day conversation.

But soiled Band-Aids, usually strewn on the floor of the shower stall in gyms and such, just totally gross me out. I don't know what it is or why, but they do. What was important here, however, is that Nika not only *knew* this, but had kept a *record* of it! (All right, I take back what I said about her never using her classical archaeology degree.)

I put the envelope in my pocket and continued my probe.

An envelope with just the letter *K* on the front was interesting. It had the February cover of *Horse Play* magazine folded up inside, the one that everyone in Texas had been talking about, with our own Melissa Song doing piaffe, which is a sort of trot in place, on her best horse, the horse she hoped would take her to the Olympics. Someone had burned through two places in the photograph.

I'm not exactly familiar with cigarettes, never having smoked, but it looked deliberate, maybe because they were precisely round burns, not just irregular brownish smudges as if someone had accidentally done it. The burns had obliterated Melissa's face and—get this—her crotch. God, it made me cringe.

Then I saw an envelope with Lola's name. Inside it was a cassette tape labeled *Copy*. I went to slide the tape into the pocket of my shift, but instead it fell.

I bent down for it, but my back sort of popped, as if the climbing that I'd done was maybe more than I ought to have tried. I played it smart and squatted.

And that was when I saw the garment bag that was lying way in the back on the floor. Actually, not lying but scrunched there.

This had to be it, the shadbelly and the vest, the FEI clothes. Except that I couldn't just walk out the door with the thing slung over my arm. I mean, I could, but I would need nerves of steel to pull it off. I knew I didn't have nerves of steel, so why try?

I know you're thinking I was obsessed with these clothes and you're right, I was. But it wasn't an idle obsession. I had the feeling that these clothes would prove something, although I have to admit I didn't know what. But obsessions aren't reasonable things, are they?

Almost without hesitating, I grabbed the garment bag and found myself leaning over the deck and dropping it over the side. It made a soft *whump*, but nothing that would have attracted attention from the crew downstairs. And the bag was sand-colored, so it wouldn't be seen from the road.

I congratulated myself, patted the tape inside my pocket, and prepared to start down the stairs again, this time drawn by the exquisite smell of cumin and cilantro. Jim Rockford, I decided, had *nada* on me.

But acoustics in the hills being what they are, the sound of cars, many *many* cars, heading right this way, filled my ears. I could forget about getting to my truck before they arrived. I raced down and out and ran toward the barn, gaining it just as the first car in what appeared to be a lengthy procession was pulling up.

Barn. It is such an inelegant word. Let me substitute, therefore, stable. Or, wait a minute, that doesn't quite do it for this place. I should use the plural, *stables*, as Nika always did.

She'd pulled out all the stops where her horses were concerned. There was a cathedral ceiling and a patterned brick floor. There were massive oak stalls with bright brass plaques identifying the inhabitants. There were little brass spigots shaped like fox masks in front of each stall, and oaken, brass-bound buckets, too. It was as if one of the famous stables overseas—the queen's, maybe—had been magically relocated here in Texas.

Nika used to like to give tours. Newcomers always said the same thing, too. One word: *Whoa!*

Need I add that the horses herein housed were spectacular, well-bred, muscular, and huge. They were also incredibly clean. Their coats glistened and their manes and tails were tangle free. All errant hairs around the muzzle and such had been shaved away. Even their hooves were polished. And this was the way they looked every single day of their lives.

Plum, on the other hand, and I daresay most of the horses in the world, only approached this state on the morning of a show. I use the word *approach*, you'll note. I don't think most *people* have ever been this clean.

The horses nickered for attention and I walked along the aisle, stroking as I went along and wishing I'd carried some carrots.

Then I heard, "There you are," behind me and I turned to see Jeet. "Glad you're feeling better, hon," he said, and closed his arms around me. When we finished swaying together, Vince had caught up to him.

"Whoa!" Vince said, looking around.

Jeet had seen the place before. He said, "Why'd you park down on the road?"

I thought fast. "Because I'm driving Mother. Can you imagine if anybody hemmed me in?"

Jeet looked at me admiringly. He told Vince, "You should see her wheel that truck of hers around."

Jeet likes the fact that I am competent. It turns him on. Jeet likes nothing better than to see me, all grubbed up, running breakneck for the shower. It's when I come out, newly scrubbed, that he's especially amorous. The problem here, of course, is that I'm usually speeding around because we're supposed to be somewhere already.

Of course sometimes I get lovey-dovey when he's not in the mood himself. Like when he's working on something, hunched up in front of the computer screen. Or worse, when he's cooking.

One time I was reading a magazine that said that women who were overweight just weren't getting enough sex. I told Jeet this. I mean, it's a harmless enough thing to say.

He was measuring the flour that he'd already sifted several times. He said, "Uh-huh," in an absentminded kind of way.

"Did you hear me?" I continued. "It says that over-weight women are sex-starved."

He ran a spatula over the surface of the flour, leveling it. A fine white drift of snow surrounded him, like an aura.

"Sex-starved," I said as he frowned at the cup and dumped it into the bowl. Because so far, I wasn't sure that he was listening.

Anyway, this is the scene that I have locked in my mind: Jeet putting the cup down. Dusting the flour from his hands. Looking at me. And saying, all very matter-of-fact, "Robin. If you're ravenously hungry right now, fine, because I haven't moistened the dry ingredients. On the other hand, the oven temperature is exactly where I want it, so if you're only moderately hungry . . ."

Hey. I was only reading an article, not attempting to seduce the man. And even if I had been, what could be more of an *an*aphrodisiac than to have the guy tell you that his dry ingredients hadn't been moistened. I mean, really.

Now, however, the vision of me behind the wheel of the Mother Ship was doing its stuff. Jeet reaches for me, pulls me close. Oh, God, but I love this man. And we're twelve years married, too.

Vince says, "Uh . . ." and Jeet and I, like teenagers who've been caught in the act, abruptly pull apart.

"So," Jeet addresses him, his voice especially serious, "how goes the investigation, Vince?"

I can't believe he's been with Vince all morning and hasn't asked him this, can you? But Vince doesn't seem to find this weird. "They're still poking around, you know," he says.

"Poking around?" I say, putting my face right in front of his.

"Yeah, you know." Vince averts his eyes.

"Poking where?"

"All over. But there's, like, an opinion that they're forming."

"An opinion?"

"You know, that it was an accident, the whole thing." He looks back at me at last.

"An accident?" My eyes get big, and Vince, therefore, begins to wax dramatic.

"Tell you what, Robin. I'll bet you the killer is right here, right now, on the premises."

I look at Jeet, but he is otherwise occupied. He is reading the contents label on a half-used sack of feed.

"I'd agree with that," I said, thinking about the folks that are right now back in Nika's house. "So choose. Who?"

"Choose," Vince says, strutting up and down the aisles with his chin propped by his hand. He stops. "Okay, I chose." And he stands there. All he needs is a deer-stalker hat.

"Do I have to close my eyes or what?" I ask.

He gives one of those laughs that's nearly a cough, and then he opens the door to Haarlem's stall. The big Dutch Warmblood has been eating hay. Now the horse looks startled, wisps sticking out from the edges of his mouth. It's as if he's saying, *Who? Me?*

"I don't get it," I announce.

Vince closes the stall door. Haarlem continues to stare. "Think about it. The coroner, he finds the imprint of a horse's shoe on Nika's forehead, nail marks and all. And that blow was the cause of death. And this horse"—he gestures at Haarlem again—"his hoofprints were closer to the markings than any of the other horses were."

First of all, all this stuff about the imprint of a horse's shoe is news to me. I agree with Haarlem, who blows out, making a sort of raspberry before going back to munching. "Oh, right," I say, and then, without thinking first, "And what about Lola?"

"What about her?" Jeet asks, wandering to my side.

Fortunately, Vince ignores what *both* of us have said, countering, "They're pretty sure she was killed by a horse, Robin. I can understand why you wouldn't want to deal with that, but it's true, case closed."

And maybe it would have been, except for one thing: down at the end of the aisle, past Jeet, past Vince, I hear movement. Not animal movement, but something that sounds—don't ask me how I know, but I do—like people movement. Or *person* movement anyway. As if someone had been listening to this whole exchange.

CHAPTER 5

For some unknown reason, Jeet has me following him home from the Cliffside Farm wake. Probably to keep me from what he thinks of as speeding. The fact is, I don't speed. I don't think Mother—a senior citizen, after all—is up to anything past fifty-five. Everything just feels fast in this truck, that's all. So whenever Jeet has to travel in it—and that's as infrequently as he can manage—he is always on my case about how fast I'm going.

I can see why he thinks that. Because Mother creaks and groans and rattles as if she doesn't think she's able to make the trip. Whenever I shift, for instance, there's a low, ratchety moan. And sometimes I can't shift at all. Whatever is in there—a little bitty opening or something; I mean, I'm not mechanically inclined—just stays shut. I have to get up under the hood in order to fix it. But if you finesse the Mother Ship, you can, I've discovered, keep this from happening. Pretty much. You have to finesse the Mother Ship into just about everything, in other words.

Which is probably why I like this truck. It's horselike in that regard. Responsive if you know the proper, sometimes idiosyncratic, aids.

And it's a true Texas truck, which means not just that the license plate identifies it as same, it means that it contains the necessary dashboard accoutrements. It has a flashlight that doesn't work. It has two or three pop-top cans, empty, (in my case diet Coke as opposed to Lone Star beer). And it has an oft-used roll of duct tape, and grimy old work gloves, an unmatched pair. It also has a bumper sticker, courtesy of its previous owner, announcing that it is *Insured by Smith & Wesson* and a gun rack where I keep my whips to prove it.

I never feel tinier or daintier than when I'm driving Mother.

And, because I'd presented her to a disbelieving workperson at one of those aforementioned auto-sound-installation outlets just last year, she also has a cassette player.

I popped the tape labeled *Copy* in and waited.

And waited.

And waited.

Nothing. I looked down, swerving slightly as I did so and pressed eject. I tried inserting it again. More nothing. Finally, even though I was supposed to be following Jeet, I pulled over and tugged at the cassette itself.

Of course I got spaghetti. It looked as though nearly half the tape had unspooled.

And meanwhile, up ahead, Jeet, too, had pulled over to the side. He was craning to see out of his rearview mirror. So I couldn't rewind it right then.

I pulled into traffic again, smiling to reassure Jeet, smiling even though I was almost clipped by a passing Beamer.

My first response was to want to yell at the guy, really chew him out. I mean, it does get rid of any built-up steam to do that. But one time, when I did just that, it turned out that it was my hay man I was screaming at. Prior to which event he'd been delivering gorgeous bales of coastal at below market price. And following which event he wasn't interested in selling me his hay for any amount of money.

And besides, Jeet, who is the original Mr. Nice Guy, wouldn't approve. And also, the car in question was a long time gone by the time I'd reached this point in my reasoning.

I waved, Jeet waved back. We were on our way again.

Which gave me time to consider Vince's accident story. Could it really be true? Not that I am any expert, but it *felt* as if there'd been a murder to me. There was that call to our house, for instance. A call to Jeet or me. A call that I'd get to listen to as many times as I wanted when we finally got home and saw the little red message light beckoning to us.

Except that I caught the light at MLK and Route 973 and watched Jeet drive on, probably figuring that I'd be okay from this point on. And when I walked inside, Jeet had already finished listening to the answering-machine tape.

"Who was it?" I asked.

"Nobody." Jeet was readjusting the machine so that it would erase the tape.

"I want to hear," I say, "really."

"There's no reason to hear," he points out.

"But . . ."

"What's the matter?" he asks.

He looks at me, I mean really, genuinely looks at me. My nose pinches at the bridge, as if I'm going to cry. There is a moment when I almost tell him everything, about Lola, about the call, about all the things I've done since this whole thing happened.

But before I can say anything, he pulls me up against him and strokes my hair and keeps telling me he's sorry, that he should've realized how this would affect me, how I've been so brave, acting as though nothing much had happened while, deep down inside, I was frightened, grieving, yearning for comfort and solace and love.

The next morning was Tuesday, but it had that Sunday feel anyway, in that we were slower than usual to rise. In fact, I was just cozying my backside against Jeet's when, outside, Plum began beating on her water trough, a reminder.

I went outside in just a nightgown and the flats I'd worn the day before. Already, the heat was starting to bear down on us.

"Hey, girl," I said, scratching the underside of Plum's head. This—the long deep crevice there—is Plum's favorite spot. She screwed her head this way and that way so that she could get me scratching where she itched the most.

Then, as if she'd suddenly remembered, she jerked back as if I'd been trying to distract her. She pawed and tossed her head and whinnied in a feathery kind of way. Then she stood by the place where her feed pail would be hung once I got it out there.

I took the cue. And while she ate her grain I got the hose going, then heaved a couple of flakes of coastal, too. Later I would groom her. Then I'd fill a wheelbarrow with her droppings. Sappy as it sounds, I loved the dailiness of all of this.

When I got inside, Jeet was standing there in his underwear, coffeepot in hand. He poured a mugful for me. I waited until he left and I heard the shower to replay the tape of the killer calling my house. But Jeet was right. It was nobody. Just a hang-up, not even any breathing.

When I walked into the bedroom, Jeet was making

little stacks of clothes: T-shirts, shorts, polo shirts.
"What's going on?" I said.

He glanced up. "I told you."

"Told me what?"

"About the Florentine Festival," he says.

"What Florentine Festival?"

"Robin. The three-day schmear that I have to cover
for the paper. In South Padre. Tomorrow. The Florentine—"

It was starting to sound vaguely familiar. I think I'd
even written it on the calendar. "You mean the spinach
thing?" I interrupt him.

"Exactly. And see? You learned it. You said you
never would."

What he means is the little mini-course he'd had to
give me: Introduction to Food Terminology. So that I
wouldn't sound like a know-nothing at some of the deals
we had to attend. What deals? Well, like a caviar tast-
ing. And like judging an art contest where all the pieces
were made of food. Except that the one that won was
made of tallow. Who, I ask you, would consider that a
food? I mean, can you imagine serving tallow sand-
wiches? Tallow casserole? Anyway, I have learned.
"Florentine means spinach," I recite. "Véronique
means grapes." And the word *Véronique* made me
think of Veronika. Easy to remember. Sour grapes.

"Good girl," Jeet says. Then he pecks at my cheek
and departs. Then he pops back in and says, "Remember, we have to do a restaurant tonight. You can meet
me there. We'll go early, as soon as they open." He
calls out the address and I write it down, stick it with
a magnet up on the fridge.

What all did I need to do today?

I guess you're wondering what it is that I *do* do. I

mean, if money is so tight and all, why is it that I don't work?

First, there isn't that much call for an overthirty over-weight phys. ed. major, I mean, no niche that I exactly fit right into. I mean, can you imagine me applying to teach an aerobics class? They would look at me and think I was making a joke.

I have, however, tried other forms of employ.

None has been successful, however. I sold cosmetics door-to-door and got fired because I didn't *wear* cosmetics while I was trying to hawk them. Then I proof-read for a local magazine and was great at it until, shortly after hiring me, they went out of business.

Plus, both those times, Jeet and I had to hire some-one to do the stuff I now ordinarily do. The horse work. And the housework. And the laundry and the shopping. And actually all of the routine maintenance of the place. Like the mowing and the weeding and the leaky faucets and loose chair legs and whatnot. Can you imagine what we had to pay someone to do all of this? And *finding* someone wasn't easy either. So it makes sense for me not to work at a real job. Anyway, I am not without my talents. I can, for instance, make a bed with a cat still in it. But you see, this is not what anyone could call a highly marketable skill.

Which doesn't get me closer to figuring out what it is that I need to do today.

I need to listen to that tape. I need to ride. I need to . . . my pencil pauses and then, as if it's automatic writing or something, I see that I've listed Ron.

Ron.

I also had to see about Lola. I mean, if the police have decided that this whole thing was an accident, why had they held her? Why were they holding her still? Or had Lola been so humiliated that she was hiding out someplace?

But right then I kept coming back to Ron. I kept thinking that he's guilty, somehow, no matter what the police or anybody had to say. And he'd somehow blamed Lola.

I decided to go with the flow and call him without delay.

I expected, I guess, that when he answered, he'd incriminate himself, if only through background noises, like ice tinkling in martini glasses, or lilting feminine laughter. Like maybe he'd be there with the three Chicana caterer's helpers or something.

And Ron would be like that, too. He'd want someone eighteen or nineteen, tops. And definitely someone who didn't ride. I mean, that's the way it always is, a kind of seesaw, where, if the woman is obsessed with horses, the man is hostile to them. I can name you a hundred couples who are just like that. Well, think of Jeet and me. Not that I'm obsessed, and not that he's hostile, but the *pattern* is there. The pattern, the seesaw with me up and him down. When had Ron ever been seen at a horse show? When had anyone so much as seen him in the barn? At this point, while the Cliffside phone had begun to ring, I'd concluded that Ron had probably hated Nika. That he'd been wanting to bash her head in for a long, long time.

But when Ron answered, his voice was so sorrowful, so depleted somehow, that I ended up telling him how sorry I was, how I hadn't had a chance to talk to him at the wake, but how I wanted him to know . . . etc.

At which point he began to weep. "She was my baby," he said. "She was my little girl."

"Well, I, you know, I . . ." was about my end of the conversation.

"I loved her. She was my baby." He seemed caught in this loop. "Oh, Veronika," he'd say, as if he were a one-man Greek chorus. And then the baby part again.

At this point I'd have been enchanted by anything other than this—a quick summary of their entire marriage, even.

Ah, but then I realize what, in the cosmic scheme, is going on here.

Of course.

What is going on here is that this is my due. This is the penalty that's heaped upon people like me, people who steal black leather books from churches.

I am humbled. I listen to the entire thing.

Eventually I did get off the phone. I immediately rushed to my truck, hoping fervently that the Texas sun hadn't caused the unraveled tape to merge with the vinyl of the seat covers. It looked okay. I took it in and, with a pencil, got the thing rewound. Then I began to search for our tape player, realizing, finally, that Jeet must have taken it in to work.

No matter. There was an even better one at Lo's. I could ride over there and kill two birds with one stone. But then again, given the time it would take to groom and saddle and then actually get there, I decided to drive.

The place seemed abandoned, though it was probably my mind that was making me look at it that way. But it did. It seemed so, I don't know, Lolaless.

I opened the front gate, drove inside, closed the gate, and made my way toward the house.

I was sure that at the house, I would have to use my key. I can't tell you what it's like, after a hundred times of *not* having to use it—with all that that represents—

to have to do so. It was as though Lola, not Nika, had died.

One of Lola's horses was in the paddock drinking. He bore a saddle mark. I brightened a bit, knowing that Suzie had worked him at least.

But the front door wasn't locked. In fact, the latch hadn't even caught because it had creaked open at my very touch. My first thought was, Someone's in here! Then I realized that I was being a dope.

I went right to the tape recorder and plopped the cassette into place. Then I pulled the hassock close to it and hunched forward, listening.

The voice on the tape was wobbly because of the rewinding, but it was Nika's voice, thanking whomever for holding the line. The bitch, I thought. Did she tape every single conversation? And did she keep them all? Or just the ones that had some dirt, something she could use?

And then my heart stopped. It was Lola's voice now, wobbly, too, but unmistakably there on the tape with Nika's: "I just wanted you to know, Veronika, that you'll pay for this tasteless little escapade of yours."

Lola's voice sounded hard, metallic. And cold. Murderously cold.

But it got worse after Nika laughed. It said, "You bitch. Somebody ought to smash your head in. Someone ought to grind your face into pulp."

I clicked it off. I let myself absorb this. Then I rewound it and played it a second time.

Oh, God.

Lola's voice had me mesmerized. It was hers, but it was not hers. What I'm thinking of is this phenomenon—and it has a name, but I can't remember what— where someone goes off the deep end and even their facial features change. It was Vince who had told me about the phenom, whatever it was. Listening now, I could picture Lola's face doing that, turning from beautiful to threatening, maybe even ugly.

". . . Somebody ought to smash your head. . . ."

And further on down, Lola, not Nika, laughs. Not the way Lola usually does. Not the way she does with me. Not a laugh at all, really, but a threat.

Wow.

I hit rewind again.

And then the room seemed to get smaller, crowd in upon me even. I felt scalding hot. And I was afraid. I mean deeply afraid. All of these sensations came separately, just as I'm relaying them, but it was what they added up to that mattered. What they added up to was this: That there was someone, right this minute, right now, in the room with me. Someone standing close, too. I could feel the person's presence, a kind of heat.

CHAPTER 6

I mean it. Someone was there. And I, frozen into position on that hassock, could now hear the proof of it.

My breath.

Someone else's breath.

My breath.

Someone else's.

I was tingling with the knowledge that I had to do something. Counterattack.

And all I could think of was this old gym teacher of mine, Miss Barr, telling the class—I'm talking high school here—that we should always carry a hatpin with us just in case. I didn't even know what a hatpin was. Nobody I knew ever wore a hat. But in any case, right now I wished that I had such a pin.

And then I thought about karate. I mean, I had studied it some. Enough to know that just maintaining an air of menace was important.

With that I war-whooped, launching myself off the hassock, swiveling as I did so into a pretty good opening stance.

Except that it was Lola standing there, Lola, totally disheveled and in a pink chenille bathrobe that looked as though it had been totally worn out more than a decade ago. And she was holding something, clutching it to her bosom, in fact. It was not a hatchet, nor a gun. It was a half-gone bag of Oreos.

At this point I shook myself out of my absurd posture with pretty much the same air that I'd used to retrieve the parking ticket off my windshield. Not that Lola acknowledged that anything in my behavior was awry.

I let my eyes sort of casually rove around the room. Over the empty Häagen-Dazs carton. The near empty bag of M&M's.

Meanwhile, in the background, the tape hissed, waiting to be replayed. Lola reached past me, punching the power button off.

"You had to do this, didn't you, Robin," she says. "You had to hammer this thing into the ground."

"Oh, God," I respond. "This tape is why you were under arrest."

"Under arrest? What are you talking about?"

"The police. I was here, remember?"

"I was questioned, Robin. Not arrested. There's a big difference."

"But I saw them take you away."

"For questioning."

"So somebody gave them a copy of this tape," I said. "Ron, probably."

"I'm sick to death of this tape," Lola said. "This tape has ruined my life."

"Still," I said, "how could they hold you so long just for questioning? It's unconstitutional, isn't it?"

"What do you mean, long? I was there an hour, two hours, max."

"No way, Lola. Because I went down there, and the cop at the reception desk told me that I couldn't see you."

"Probably because I was gone."

"Gone where?"

"Someplace. Gone. A movie."

"Oh, sure, a movie," I said, as sarcastically as I could. I watched her for a moment. Then I eased up. "Lola, this is stupid. Do you expect me to believe that you didn't call me? Me? Your nearest and dearest? Your . . ."

I'd have gone on, but Lola had begun to weep. She threw herself facedown onto the sofa, Oreos and all. I could hear the cellophane squeal as her shoulders jerked around on top of the bag.

What had I said? I reached down and tried to undo whatever it was by stroking her hair.

It sort of worked. Lola raised herself, got into a sitting position, and sniffled. I ran and fetched a dish towel. I handed it to her and then we both stared at each other. Finally she broke the stare by fishing out another Oreo, miraculously unscathed. She separated it, then raked her front teeth across the icing.

"Why didn't you call?" I said.

"Look, Robin, you don't know everything. That tape, for instance. Way back when I first called Nika. After . . . you know. Way back then she taped me and she turned the thing over to the police. She accused me right then of threatening her, the bitch."

"You mean they questioned you then?"

"Yes."

"So of course they thought of you this time, too."

"Yes."

"But," I still wondered, "why didn't you call?"

"I was too devastated," she said.

"By being arrested?"

"*Questioned.* And no, not that. Just having all this stuff brought up again." Her eyes began to well anew.

"But a movie, Lola, I don't know. That sounds so . . ."

"I don't care how it sounds, Robin, for God's sake."

"What did you see?"

"Reversal of Fortune."

"About the Von Bulow thing?"

"Yes."

"That isn't even playing anywhere," I said.

"It's at the Dobie."

"And anyway," I said, "that's so incriminating."

Lola rolled her eyes.

I kept going. "Well, if you weren't in jail," I demanded, "why weren't you at the funeral?"

"I *was* at the funeral," she insisted.

"I didn't see you."

"I didn't see *you*. Robin, what is this?"

"I'm not sure. I just know I didn't see you and I was upstairs in the choir loft checking everybody out."

Lola sighed. "I was kind of in hiding," she said, "but I was there." And then she launched into a pretty fair imitation of the minister. She clapped the cookie bag over her heart, and her eyes aiming skyward, she intoned, "She was a Thoroughbred. She had great heart."

I laughed. "God, I know. Wasn't that gross?"

"Especially since we all know that she didn't have a heart at all. She had a charcoal briquet in there where her heart should have been." The fire was back in Lola's eyes.

"Why were you hiding?" I asked her.

She turned away.

"Lo?"

She started crying again. "You didn't see him?" she sniveled.

"See who?"

"Cody. He was there." Her lower lip began to quake. Then she just crumbled, sinking to the floor, her shoulders heaving, her hair falling into her eyes.

I reached for the dish towel again and sat on the floor

beside her. I traded her the towel for the Oreos and she began blowing her nose and alternately moaning and rocking.

I put my arm across her shoulder and said, "Lola, Lola," as if she were a child.

And the next thing that I knew, she was telling me that she loved Cody, loved him, that she'd never stopped.

I felt awful. As if I'd never been her friend at all. Because I'd never even suspected this. "I didn't know," I said. "I mean, I knew you still cared, but I didn't think it was, you know, this much."

"Neither did I," Lola answered. "But that tape and thinking about all that and then *seeing* him. Oh, God, *seeing* him."

She got up and moved across the room to one of the bookcases. She rooted around behind it and then she pulled out an enormous painted sign. She held it up. It read: LOCO FARMS.

"We were going to turn this place into a really incredible show barn," she sobbed. "God, we had plans. You wouldn't believe it, Robin."

Actually, the part that I couldn't believe was that Cody, a classic *He Doesn't* if I ever saw one, was going to participate in any of this.

But then she started in on the particulars, and it turned out that they did have plans. Plans that might make money, too, with overnight stabling and an indoor arena and everything.

"Why do you need Cody for this?" I asked. "Why can't you do it on your own?"

"Because I'm broke, that's why. Do you think that horses are selling now? I'm lucky that I can eventually pay my bills."

I remembered the trophy's contents—*Final Notice,*

Overdue—and even looked over where the trophy stood. It was empty now. "Cody has money?"

"He's not Ron Ballinger, but he's got enough. Robin, you are so *stupid* sometimes. I mean, can you really believe that I'd be out there grubbing an arena out of nothing with my bare hands if I could afford to have someone come in and just do it? Do you think I'd be putting up my own fencing or building my own jumps?"

She had a point there.

"Robin," she went on, "I've had to sell things."

"What things?"

"The tractor, for one. Don't you remember how good this place used to look when I had a tractor?" She squinted at me. "You don't remember, do you?" Then she threw up her hands. "You are so oblivious," she said.

When I drove away, I debated whether or not to carry my investigation into all of this any further. I mean, Lo was free. And what did I care whether the police thought it was a murder or an accident or what. And anyway, if I was so stupid and oblivious, what good could it possibly do for me to continue anyway.

I know, you think my feelings were hurt by what Lola said, but that isn't true. I am oblivious sometimes, and Jeet has said so, too. Except that Jeet thinks it's because I'm concentrating so hard on one thing that I don't see something else. And that's somehow nicer than the way Lola put it.

And I know she's distraught right now. I know that. But I still can't help feeling just a little bit—what?— *stung* by what's just gone on.

Like, if Lola's my best friend, how come I didn't know about the whole business of her threatening Nika until now? And more importantly friendship-wise, how come I didn't know how she still felt about Cody until now? And if Lola's my best friend, how come I didn't know how badly she needed money? Maybe—I think this is the part that left me feeling bruised—I thought of Lola as my best friend and she, meanwhile, thought of me as some casual acquaintance.

In the middle of all of this self-flagellation, I remembered that stupid garment bag. Because if it did contain the riding clothes I thought it did, I just couldn't let it stay out there to molder. An FEI outfit probably ran a thousand dollars, if not more.

So I made my way to Cliffside yet again, retrieving the bag without incident. On the way home I was thinking, No wonder so many houses are robbed. I mean, here I was, in one of the ritziest neighborhoods in Austin, and look at what I'd gotten away with. It was pretty amazing, really. Of course, if my skin were bronzed or darker, if I drove a low rider with fuzzy dice hanging off the mirror, then I'd probably have been nabbed before I got out of the truck.

There was no justice in the world.

At home I found the light on the answering machine flashing. It was Jeet. "Don't forget," he says. "Los Dos, six o'clock." It took me a beat to realize that he was reminding me about the restaurant review. Which should be going down, by my watch, in less than an hour.

Needless to say, I dropped the garment bag over a chair and bolted for the shower. I weighed the odds while I was in there. I could be late or I could go into town with my hair wet. The latter, I decided. Wet hair Jeet can handle. Late he cannot. Then I thought about the name of the restaurant, Los Dos. The Two. Los Dos what?

All of this in-the-shower thinking was an attempt to distract myself. I mean, as silly as it sounds, I hate to take a shower when I'm home alone. It must be fifteen years or more since I saw *Psycho*, but I always think about that movie when I'm in the shower. What I do is, I soap one eye at a time. I don't know what this is supposed to accomplish, except that it would enable me to *see* Norman Bates before he does me in. But I'm serious. I am really scared when I'm taking a shower.

On the other hand, the minute I'm dripping onto the bath mat, I feel safe. Such are the wonders of the human mind, I was thinking as I reached for my toothbrush.

And then I heard something downstairs fall. Something real. I pulled my dirty clothes back on—my clean ones were in the bedroom—and I picked up an ancient aerosol can of hairspray. And I stood there, ready. In fact, I was already imagining myself blasting Ron Ballinger right between the eyes.

But at the same time, of course, I was hoping, fondly, that I hadn't really heard a thing. Except that I did. I know I did.

And now, right now, I hear something even closer. Something, yes, right in the hall. Something like someone out there trying very hard not to be heard.

I rev myself up the way I used to before going onto the lacrosse field. Kill or be killed, I'm committed, I think.

I turn the knob of the bathroom door and there's a loud click as the thing unlocks. A click that whoever is out there must have heard.

I wait. I haven't let go of the knob, so now all I have to do is pull.

And I do, slowly, slowly, slowly.

And then *bam!* Someone pushes on the door and it

practically breaks my wrist. But that doesn't mean I'm
not prepared, because, by crackee, I am. I push down
on the button on the top of the hairspray can. I scream
like a banshee, "Ay-yeeee."

And he does, too, waving his arms as though the
killer bees are here and upon him.

Fortunately the little hole on the can was all gunked
up from lack of use, so he wasn't blinded.

"Cody, I thought you were—" I began, and then
I stopped myself. "Well, maybe you are. . . ." I
went on.

"What?" He is dusting himself off even though there
isn't a drop of anything on him, I swear. Men are ba-
bies.

"A murderer."

"Oh, yeah? And is that why you left your keys in the
door?" He hands them to me and I pocket them sheep-
ishly. But then he gets into it, waxes dramatic. "I *am*
a murderer," he says, looking me right in the eye. But
Cody has always had a flair for this sort of speech. And,
sure enough, he goes on to say that what he has killed
is his relationship with Lola, the only relationship that
has ever mattered.

"Oh, right," I say. "And how about the one with
Nika Ballinger and God knows how many others? Just
imagine how Lola must have felt, seeing you, seeing
Nika, seeing her shish-kabobed like that."

"I was a jerk, okay?" he admits. "But I still do love
Lo. I mean, *really* love Lo. And I'm just wondering,
you know, how she feels about me."

LoCo Farms, I remember. "Is that why you came
back?"

"That's why."

"And you just happened to arrive on the day of Nika's funeral."

"Right," he says. "Just a stroke of luck."

I look at him long and hard. He looks back at me. If he were a killer, would he be able to do that? Maintain eye contact, I mean?

"Cody," I say, "I just don't know what to do. For all I know, you really could be a vicious murderer. I think I should call the police."

"Lo was right about you," he says, laughing.

"Right how?" I ask, drawing myself up so that I'm taller, about to his shoulders. (Jeet isn't terribly tall, just a shade taller than me. Which is great, because I don't have to spend the majority of my life feeling insignificant, the way tall men like Cody make me feel.)

"You crack me up," he says. "Like if I were a vicious murderer, I would just step aside and let you make that call. In fact, I would hand you the phone. You're so naive."

"You broke into my house," I tell him.

"I told you, the keys were in the door."

"Still, you could have knocked."

"I pounded repeatedly," he says.

"But you came all the way upstairs," I argue.

Cody reaches for me, grabs my shoulders, puts his face practically on top of mine. "Robin." He gives me a little shake. "Think about it. For all I knew, you were in here hurt or dead."

I try to squirm away.

"No, really," he says. "Think about it. Your keys in the door and you don't answer . . ."

I bat his arms away. I don't want to think about it. I want life the way it used to be, when people weren't getting killed all around me or fearing that maybe I was upstairs in my own home, murdered, too.

I didn't like the way my life was suddenly turning out. I didn't like the fact that I wasn't the only one thinking there was a murderer on the loose. I didn't like being scared. I didn't like not knowing if Cody was a potential rescuer or someone intent on doing me in. I said all this or maybe whined it, I don't know.

Cody stepped back and spread his arms as wide as he could spread them in our narrow upstairs hall. "Take a look, kid. What do you think? Want to see if I'm carrying a weapon? Want to pat me down?"

In that instant I decide that Cody, with his sunburn and his ponytail and his battered cowboy boots and his faded jeans, couldn't be a murderer after all. Plus he is the perfect height for Lola, who is taller than a lot of men.

"Oh, God, it's late," I finally say. "I have to get out of these old clothes."

"But I came here to talk," Cody says.

So I consent to letting him stand in the hallway just beyond the bedroom door while I pull on panty hose and whatnot and all the while shout answers at him. I conclude by telling him—reluctantly, to be sure—that Lola still loves him.

He asks, "You sure?"

"Yes. So go on over there and declare yourself," I say, poking little gold studs into my earlobes. By the time I get them anchored, Cody is long gone.

Los Dos. It is one of those restaurants with a gimmick and in this case the gimmick is couples. This is signified by the fact that all of the tables are tables for two. Except that in addition to three boy-girl couples, there is a boy-boy couple and a girl-girl couple. And because the place is candlelit and the music is that old-time Jackie Gleason trumpet stuff, everyone is acting very couplelike indeed. Even in Austin, I tell Jeet, I don't think this ploy is commercially viable.

"I'm here to review the meal," he says, an affronted liberal.

"You do the ambience, too," I argue.

We began a skirmish over whether or not the ambience includes the clientele. Jeet cheated, though, filling my wineglass to the brim and waiting for the wine to hit me so that I'd shut up.

Later we walk the downtown streets, holding hands. "The vinaigrette was a tad on the bitter side," he says.

"Mmm-hmm."

"And I thought they should have served sweet butter, didn't you?"

"Mmm-hmm."

"On the other hand, the batter that they used on the appetizers, the one with the cod especially, was . . ." etc.

I was still in the mmm-hmm stage when we got back to my truck, which made Jeet decide to leave his car where it was and drive Mother home. He'd be leaving for Padre in the morning. The photographer could pick him up at home.

"Which photographer is it?" I ask. There is Greta, who allegedly has sued the paper, charging that the photo editor made an indecent proposal to her when, in fact, all he did was ask, "Do you want it horizontal or vertical?" when printing up one of her negatives. And then there is Dean, who is okay. Jeet doesn't know which one he'll draw.

"It disturbs me, though, that they didn't have Lillet in stock."

This is his favorite aperitif. "Mmm-hmm," I respond, letting him place me on the passenger side.

Then he gets in. "Where is first again?" he asks, sliding behind the wheel and fondling the Mother Ship's gearshift knob.

* * *

The house was dark and we more or less blundered into it. Not that we don't know our own house, just that things sort of build up on the floor. Like bootjacks and boots themselves and hard hats and oddments of saddlery.

But fortunately the message light is blinking and we were able to use that as a beacon.

Three messages.

The first was from Lola, and it said: "Once and for all, Robin, will you just butt out of my life? I mean, when will you learn? And it isn't just my life, it's everyone's life, it's as though you—" and then there was the beep that indicated that the message space had run out.

Next was Cody, with a message of his own. His went: "Robin, honey, you're a wonderful judge of human nature, wonderful. And I appreciate the advice. And kinky as I am, I really really enjoyed Lola coming after me with a hoof pick when I came to the door—" *Beep.*

The third message was Cody, the Sequel. "Really, kid, the whole thing was a total thrill. And in future, Robin, if you want to advise me on the next step I should take, just call my lawyer, okay? That way he can find out firsthand what you're up to, not rely on secondhand information from me." *Beep.*

"Ah," Jeet says, bending forward to kiss the back of my neck. "My little matchmaker."

CHAPTER 7

"Hey," Jeet whispered, "hey." He had his hand on my shoulder and was shaking me softly.

And that's how he got me out of the jam I was in, dream-wise. I'd been running away from everyone: Ron, Suzie, Lola, Cody. I'm not kidding. They all had implements that they were bent on using on me, too. Suzie had a hatchet and Ron had a pick, and Lola had a manure rake and Cody had a shovel.

"Must have been a good one," Jeet said. He moved so I could scoot up into something resembling upright and let his arms close around my back. "Want to talk about it?" he asked.

"Everyone was out to get me," I said. I felt him give a little laugh. "I'm serious," I insisted. "And it was very scary. Especially Suzie. I mean, she was out to kill."

"Is that the most irrational part?" he asked, and I shook my head yes.

You know about this already. The theory that that's where the true meaning of the dream can be found. Because it's the way my snooping into Nika's death has been structured, too. "Suzie, yes," I said.

"And why is that more irrational than Ron chasing you?"

Jeez, it's so hard to make these nitpicking psychoanalytical distinctions first thing in the morning, you know. But I thought. "Because Ron *is* menacing," I said. "He's big and he always seems angry and I can imagine him doing it. Suzie, though . . ." I paused to conjure her pert little face and her haircut and those freckles. "I can't imagine Suzie doing anybody any harm at all."

"And Lola? And Cody?"

"Well, they're mad at me, so that part would figure."

I felt sufficiently purged of anxiety now and I lay down on my back again.

Jeet did likewise. We both stared at the ceiling. Then Jeet said, "There's something very cold about Suzie. You remember that rabbit thing."

The rabbit thing. This was an episode last year when Jeet had dropped me off at Lo's. We came up Lola's driveway to find Suzie banging a rock down on a baby rabbit's head. She looked up and cocked her head and shrugged and said, "Horse stepped on him. Someone's gotta finish the job," and then she conked him again.

I'd forgotten about that, although, at the time, it kept popping back into my mind. And every time it did, I had an involuntary shudder of disgust. Now I felt that way again. "Why'd you have to bring that up now?" I accused.

"Because that was my introduction to Suzie. I've never felt particularly warm toward her since."

"You've never felt particularly warm toward anyone who rides," I teased.

Jeet rolled over and gave me a playful pinch. "There's you."

"Oh, yeah?" I started getting into it, jabbing at him, then trying to tickle him.

He moved into a fetal pose except that he held my

hands. He was laughing and I was laughing, too, going after him.

Then—alas—someone drove up our driveway honking. "If it's Greta, she'll know you're horny," I said. "And she'll end up adding your name to the lawsuit. She'll say you asked her if she wanted her buns toasted."

Jeet was at the window, opening it, and yelling down. "I'll be right there. Just a sec." He turned to me. "It's Dean." He slid into khakis and loafers and was gone.

Before I was even minimally presentable, I could smell the coffee and the muffins. By the time I got downstairs, Dean and Jeet had all but finished theirs. Blueberry muffins with a whipped-cream-cheese spread. Not plain cream cheese, but one with fresh-grated lemon rind blended in. "Jeet, I hate you," I said, starting on my first as they loaded the car for Padre.

My plan was to immediately get myself out of the amateur detective biz. I mean, what did I care, now that Lola was home free. Except that I kept thinking about my dream, thinking about Suzie, mostly. Could Jeet be right? What did I know about her, really? Beyond her gamine appearance, I mean.

And I am kind of suckered in by appearances. Like this boss Jeet once had. I actually liked her until Jeet pointed out to me that everything the woman said was venomous. The fact was, because she always smiled when she talked, I thought she was joking around, you know, being sarcastic in an affectionate kind of way. Maybe I was doing the same about Suz. She did smile a lot, come to think of it, even when she was saying nasty and terrible things.

At least Nika had been blatantly dreadful. None of this "Look like the innocent flower, but be the serpent under it'' stuff. Once more, that business with Melissa Song popped into my head. The way Nika had resented how well she rode. The way she'd tried to have her disqualified.

But back to Suzie. Had Suzie been smiling in my dream?

But then—because Suzie was the irrational part of my dream and because that photograph of Nika was the most irrational part of the murder investigation, I started thinking about those FEI clothes again.

Who did I know who even owned FEI clothes? I wasn't sure there was anyone I knew—I mean, knew to say hello to—who rode on that level. Because dressage in Texas is still in its infancy. Or maybe I should just say Austin, because in Houston there was Melissa Song, natch, and a handful of others.

Oh, yes, Melissa had come a long, long way. It was rumored that she now had a sponsor, a rich anonymous person who footed her bills. Well, if anyone deserved such a person, Melissa did. All this and now she was a serious Olympic contender, too, the first—and maybe the only—Native American in competitive dressage.

Well, one thing was for sure. Nika, even in her sylph state, wasn't wearing Melissa's itty-bitty FEI clothes. But she was wearing someone's and I still wanted to know whose. Because it wasn't as though Reiner Klimke or Katerina Schwetman was going to call Nika Ballinger out of the blue and say, ''Nika, baby, wanna wear my clothes?''

I know you're probably thinking that Veronika Ballinger was rich enough to buy her own clothes, right? Well, if that was the case, I wanted to know that, too, although I doubted it because just ordering them would have activated the rumor mill. Someone, like the local tack-store owner, for instance, would have heard.

But maybe the answer was right under my nose. Maybe, for instance, I could look inside the garment bag that I'd purloined and there they'd be. Maybe they'd even have name tags sewn in, so the ownership question could be solved once and for all.

Except that I couldn't remember where I'd put the bag. I knew I hadn't hung it up, although eventually I did go around checking all the doorknobs and the coat tree and even the closets. I had draped it somewhere. Like the back of the couch? No. The back of any of our chairs? No again. Finally, I'd exhausted every possibility and turned my attention elsewhere. I mean, wherever it was, the bag wasn't going anyplace, was it?

I changed into my breeches and stood sideways in front of the mirror contemplating my belly. If I held it in really tight, I actually looked all right. Standing, that is. When I brought my leg up, the way you have to when you're riding, I looked really fat.

What would I look like if I didn't ride, didn't shovel horse poops every day, didn't throw hay? I would probably weigh three times as much. Didn't all of my activity count for anything? My God, how did these pencil-thin women you see walking around do it?

Why didn't the horse industry make control-top riding breeches? I couldn't be the only porker in dressage history. (Actually, in dressage history, I am not even a speck, but hey! I was working myself into a major depression here, and reminding myself of my own insignificance was part of the process.)

Nature cooperated, too. Just when I was going to step outside and put my tack on Plum, the sky opened up and buckets—I mean buckets—of rain came pouring down.

This doesn't happen much in Texas. In Texas, usually, the ground gets so dry that huge gaping cracks open up. Around Austin, anyway.

But I'm getting off the subject. My point when I first began musing was that Texas is usually bone dry. It rains in winter and that sends the furnacelike summer away. And then it rains in spring and that brings the beautiful wildflowers out. Any other kind of rain in between, you can forget.

Except for today, when I'm standing on the porch all ready to ride, catching an occasional glimpse of Plum in her shelter pretty much snug and dry.

I called Wanda, a local riding instructor, and asked if I could come over to her indoor arena for a lesson. She suggested four o'clock and I agreed. I don't usually do that, because Jeet and I can't really afford it, but I was—I don't know how else to explain it—desperate to ride, desperate to clear my mind the way only time in the saddle can clear it. And in this rain, what else could I do? I mean, usually Lo and I serve as grounds people—you know, standing on the ground while the other person's riding, saying "Yes, that's good," or "No, you need more impulsion," or "Yes, his legs are crossing," or "No, they aren't"—for each other, but now, in addition to the downpour, my grounds person was totally hacked off at me.

Plus Wanda had taught Suzie, too, and could maybe cast the deciding vote in the matter of whether or not Suz was a covert murderess who had offed her former employer, Veronika Ballinger.

It was just as well that I had this plan to get out of the house and go there, because the minute I am forced to close the kitchen door and the windows, I get cabin fever. Big-time cabin fever. Which in my case manifests itself in bingeing on food.

So I ate the remaining blueberry muffins. Then I ate half of the ravioli we had left over from dinner a few nights ago. Then I made tomato soup. Then I ate the other half of the ravioli. I looked at the clock. It was only eleven in the morning.

But this chain eating had begun. It's nothing I ever see written about. It's like, *this* food makes you want *that* food and *that* food makes you want *this* food, and it never stops. Some company should invent something you could, like, nuke your taste buds with so that this kind of thing wouldn't happen. Like a taste-deadening oral spray, maybe. Binaca Plus. Or Binaca Minus, which could get the diet-aid theme across.

Well. By the time I'd washed all the dishes that I'd dirtied, it was time to be heading out. Somehow, after this flurry of household activity, grooming Plum, even cleaning the crud out of her feet, seemed downright appealing.

After which, I tied Plum to the side of the trailer in what was now a kind of drizzly mist and put her leather head bumper on. The kind that cuts across the horse's head above the eyes, with the ears sticking out through holes? It makes horses look so dopey, but it also keeps them from banging themselves up.

Next I put the shipping wraps on her legs. Despite my efforts at toweling her, her legs were filthy and damp. Then I rolled a bandage around her tail.

I have an enormous trailer, Warmblood size. And that's because of the way Plum parks herself in there. I mean, she doesn't just walk in up to the chest bar in front the way normal horses do, okay? She stands back from it about three feet. Which means it's like transporting a horse that is three feet longer than Plum actually is.

When I had a normal-size trailer, she ballooned out over the backdoor and people started looking at me as though I ought to be reported to the ASPCA. So I sold it and bought a longer one. And with longer also comes higher. (And more expensive.) Let's put it this way: My trailer did the Mother Ship proud. Though I'd never measured, all together I was probably a forty-foot-long rig. With one ordinary horse inside.

Still, this is why her tail always had to be wrapped up tight. Because she practically sat on the butt chain and would rub her tail hairs right out.

So anyway, now she's in there. Now all I have to do is make sure I have my saddle and my bridle and my grooming tools and my checkbook and Plum's supper and I'm ready.

Once all that had been taken care of, I started warming up the truck. I meant to arrive at the instructor's house at three, groom for half an hour, walk and trot on a long rein to loosen Plum up for half an hour. It was now 1:45, about right for the trip when pulling a load. Of course I'd started wrapping and all about twenty minutes earlier.

I mention all of this because I think that unless you're actually doing it, you can't possibly realize what trailering a horse out for a lesson is like. Imagine piano lessons, except that every time you go, you have to bring your own piano, okay?

That's close.

Still, a piano is easier than a horse in a lot of ways.

A piano never has other plans, so it won't run away when you approach it.

Also, a piano won't refuse to load. A piano won't

plant its legs on the ramp and look at you as if to say, *Make me*.

Not that I currently have these problems with Plum, but I used to. Now she loads just fine. In fact, after all I've been through loading Plum, I now think of myself as a sort of one-gal crisis-intervention program in that after every single show, there's always someone who can't get his *#@! horse to enter the *#@! trailer. And that's usually the state of mind the person is in, too, *#@!. I say, "Need a hand?" and by this time they usually ask if I have a .357 Magnum they can borrow. I use the tap-tap method that was taught to Plum, and somehow it works. Partly it works because I'm calm. I'm not the one who wants to kill the horse. But actually I think it works in some mystical way, akin to the way razor blades don't rust under pyramids or something.

It was Wanda—the riding instructor, whose driveway looms—who taught me this method. Wanda is a mystic, which is on the one hand nice and on the other hand crazy making.

The tap-tap method is a case in point. I stand at the base of the ramp with horse heading inside the trailer. I tap-tap on the shoulder with my crop and—most importantly—I think about the horse going in and, voilà! You don't believe me? Try it.

Wanda is into imagery, which I don't believe she's ever studied formally, as in an advanced-poetry class. She therefore mixes metaphors or similes or whatever they are like mad. "Hold your reins as though you have eggs in your hands," she'll say. "Precious and delicate eggs that are about to hatch." Then she'll tell you, as you lengthen your horse's stride, say, to think of your hands as hoses, water streaming forth. I always get sad because my eggs have been crushed and then I lose my incentive. I tried to explain to Wanda why this is—that I'm an incredibly suggestible person—but she didn't get it.

Now she has me working on leg yield—a zigzag kind of movement that goes forward and sideways at the same time—and she tells me to let my horse's energy flow through my outside hip. Then she hollers that I'm riding with my body crooked. Well, of course I'm riding crooked. I have all this energy yanking that hip out of its socket, don't I?

Afterward she consoles me. "Boobala," she says. She calls all of her students this. It saves her from learning the names of her more occasional students. "Boobala, one day it will come to you." She knows this because of the color that she sees surrounding me, a fierce orange.

I see it, too, sort of. It's a tongue of flame hovering over my head.

It makes me happy, this. As though I've been chosen. The question, though, is when. Maybe, I think, I should hang a crystal in Plum's shelter. Wanda has them in all of *her* horses' stalls.

I ask, after I've paid her my bucks and Plum is rolling in the sand of her indoor arena, what she sees when she thinks of Suzie.

"Suzie, Suzie, yes," she says cryptically, and she shuts her eyes. "I see a deep red, a maroon almost," and then she gasps.

I imagine all those werewolf movies where the fortune-teller spies the pentagram in the poor chump's hand.

Maroon!

Wanda swallows. She is genuinely flustered now. She fans herself with a fluttery hand. "I don't understand," she says. "I was thinking of Suzie when the image of Ron entered into my mind."

"Talk about invasion of privacy," I say.

She laughs. "I mean it," she tells me, and her brow furrows and her finger wags. "It was Ron, it was his maroon, and he was surrounded by it."

"But what about Suz?" I ask.

"No color at all," she says.

"Seriously?"

"Yes. None."

"Is this normal?" I ask.

"Normal?" she responds.

I suppose that I ought to tell you that Wanda once had me and several others over for a séance, during which she tried to conjure the spirit of Alois Podhajsky. You remember Alois Podhajsky, once the head of the Spanish Riding School of Vienna. We tried very very hard that night, but Alois didn't deign to join us.

Anyway, I have this new data about Suzie to ponder as I drive home through the still-pelting rain. But I feel so good to have worked so hard, so good to have pushed Plum a bit more than I would ordinarily on my own. Oh, I know, that makes me sort of a wuss, but I find it tough working essentially on my own. I mean, in summer, it's like a hundred degrees when you wake up and the humidity hangs there like a used washcloth. So who feels like really going for it? I know, I know, I'm supposed to be disciplined enough to do that, but here's a flash. I'm not. I guess I just don't want it enough. Or I'd want it enough if we lived on the East Coast. Or in Point Barrow, Alaska. Or if I had an air-conditioned indoor arena.

I keep promising myself that I'll start getting up at five, do a super groom on Plum, and get out there and boogie, but truth be told, more often I get out there and piddle.

But progress in dressage is slow, or so everyone tells me. And that, I think, is why Lo and a lot of others go for the more revved-up version that you get when your horse is anticipating galloping full-out across some wide-open land with ten or twelve big fences on it.

All of a sudden I have a very nasty thought about Lola, about our recent ride when she got me to jump. She knows I'm afraid. So why did she do it, egg me on? Was she hoping I'd get hurt?

Okay. So in this brief trip through the rain, I've managed to move from euphoria to the pits. Usually this means that my period is on the way. I make a mental note to check my calendar once I get inside the house.

Because Lola is my friend and I know it. God, I can still remember the first time I'd ever seen her. I'd been walking around the property, which we'd just bought, and I discovered her right next door. She'd been on a tractor, shredding, which is what they call mowing down here.

A tractor. That's right, she'd brought that tractor up before. That she'd had to sell it. That she'd been reduced to doing arena maintenance the way us po' folk do.

Could the fact that Lola'd had to sell her tractor have to do with Nika's death? I mean, if she'd been pressured into selling things by Ron, say. Suppose Ron was trying to get Lola's farm, maybe to put a housing development on it?

My mind on these thoughts, I go up the hill and left into our driveway. The lightning is flaring dramatically as I round the bend. And as it flares I see a car—a beat-up something or other, maybe a Barracuda—sitting like a raven right beside the house.

Easy, easy, I'm telling myself. But even though my glimpse was maybe a nanosecond, I know that I don't recognize that car.

The car is dark.

The house is dark.

And with a forty-foot rig, there is no way that I'm able to turn around and beat a retreat.

I came to a stop and turned off all of my lights. That's a lot of lights when you're hauling a rig like mine. There are lights across the top and running lights on the sides. I mean, we're talking Christmas.

So if my visitor has any visual acuity at all, chances are that I've been seen.

I lock Mother's doors and wait and try to decide what it is I'll do if someone—maybe Ron with an ax and Suzie with a pitchfork, or whatever it was in that dream of mine— comes walking toward me. Would I mow them down with forty feet of steel? Trucks are steel, aren't they?

But no one comes. I know, though, that I'm a long way from saved. As long as I am in the driveway, whoever it is can't get out. And I'll never succeed in backing out, not in the dark, anyway. And if I go forward, he or she or they will have me.

I've got to ride Plum out of this, I figure.

I've got to ride through the woods and get to Lola's.

And because the gate that leads there is so awfully near the house, I've got to jump the fence.

Without my saddle. Without even a bridle. Because tacking up would take too long.

Oh, Lord. Not only am I thinking of jumping, which scares me to death, but I'm thinking of doing it at night and in the rain and without the minimal—nay, essential—equipment.

I unhitch Plum's lead rope and open the backdoor to the trailer to let her ease on down the ramp. She's blanketed, and in minutes the surface of the blanket is slick with rain. And now—without a stirrup to help me—I've got to mount.

I moved Plum up alongside the trailer as I stood, drenchedly, on the wheel well. It was just a giant step across the mare's back. I strained and probably would have made it had the lightning not chosen that very moment to strike.

Whatever it hit went bright yellow for a moment and then white. In the whiteness I saw a figure making its way toward me. Plum saw it, too. She whirled. And the next thing I knew, she was leaving and I was staying behind. On my back. In the driveway. Having hit the fender over the wheel well on the way down.

The lightning continued to show my probable assailant the way. He loomed over me in silhouette before he began to spin and fade as I, I suppose, began to sink into the earth a little deeper. I could hear Wanda's voice as I faded into unconsciousness, telling me that I hadn't been positive enough.

CHAPTER 8

I am walking down the aisle of a supermarket. A very expensive supermarket. The floors are mahogany and they're buffed to a high sheen, the sort of sheen that even spiked heels can't pock.

Everywhere around me, heels are clicking, though. As if there's a parade passing through in some other section of the store, like produce maybe.

Produce. Yes, it smells that way here, like ripe melons and coconut and that lemon zest.

Jeet is in produce. I don't see him, but I know that he is there. I am in the vinegar section, which alone takes up an entire aisle.

I am reaching for the bottles, marveling at them, at the labels and at the different kinds of vinegar that there are.

But Jeet has told me not to touch. One bottle, Jeet says, can cost as much as a riding lesson.

It is hard not to touch. Because, standing in the aisle and gazing up at the bottles, I'm aware that these vinegars have things immersed in them. Things that float. I squint to see.

Yes, there is one with a long sprig of dill inside.

And there is another with . . . with . . .

I have to touch the bottle. There is no other way to

91

see. I listen for Jeet, but all I hear is music, something very unsupermarkety and downright Wagnerian.

I tiptoe around the store until I spot him. He is examining a turnip, rolling it around in the palm of his hand and then hefting it as if to test its weight.

I can return to the vinegar, certain that he won't see.

I take one of the bottles down and peer at it. It is clear, the way white vinegar is. Suzie is inside. She is smiling and hacking away at a tiny replica of Cliffside Farm. I put Suz back on the shelf.

And then I catch a glimpse of Ron. There is dill or something in the bottle with him. He seems tangled in it. He is fighting to be free. The vinegar is dark, maroon in fact. Wine vinegar, for sure.

Lola and Cody are together in yet another bottle. They don't see me because they're otherwise engaged. Think Rodin here.

And then there's Nika in her shadbelly and her canary vest. She's lost her top hat, but it floats nearby. Sometimes it hovers above her, like a halo.

One more thing. Nika is dead. You can see it in her eyes.

I reach for the Nika jar and try to take it down. But several other bottles topple as I do. They hit the floor and bounce in slow-mo. Two of them break. One is plain and the person inside that one runs away before I can see who it is. Wanda is in the other bottle, the one that's all ornate. Wanda gives chase. As Wanda runs, multicolored vapors rise up in her wake.

And then the manager comes and scolds me in pantomime. The manager, who is a squat Hispanic male. He lifts me up and begins to carry me toward the street.

I am yelling for Jeet, but he is still in the turnip section and he doesn't hear. And it *is* Wagner in the background, *Die Walküre*.

* * *

"Help! Jeet, help!" I squirmed, but big round arms were holding me. And every time I hollered, rain would pound against the back of my throat and I would cough. That worked to shut me up far better than a gag.

Whoever it was, there in my driveway, patted my back and said something, but I couldn't make out what it was. I felt my mind begin to drift again, and as I yielded to the motion I realized that someone was carrying me toward the house.

I was suddenly too weary and too weak to care.

When I felt the someone take the step onto the porch, I reached up and clawed whatever flesh on his face I could and then leveraged myself onto my feet and away from him.

He was yelling my old battle cry, "Ayee!" with a curse appended in his mother tongue.

Which appeared to be Spanish.

That gave me pause. The lightning flashed and I suddenly saw his face.

It was Manuel.

Manuel. Of course. Nika's Manuel. The man whom Nika called her burro. To his face. She would actually snap her fingers when she wanted him and say, "Where's my burro? Where's my burro?" and Manuel would appear.

How he must have hated Nika, hated shining her boots as she sat there, as regally as she could muster, on her horse.

It made sense that Manuel would kill her.

He was her burro, her *por favor*. Not that she ever said *por favor* the way it's meant to be said, thank you. To Nika the term meant stable hand, the way *schwartze* has come to mean maid of any color back east.

* * *

I tried leaping off the porch and taking more or less the same route Plum had. Manuel caught hold of me though. And he held on, shouting as he closed his vise-like fingers on my wrist, "Señora, no!"

I told you about my high-school gym teacher, Miss Barr, right? Miss Barr, who, in a former life, was probably a piece of heavy construction equipment, like maybe a bulldozer. She taught us all sorts of good stuff about getting away from guys who had grabbed us, because I think being grabbed by a guy was probably the absolute worst thing she could have imagined. Anyway, one of the things she taught was that we shouldn't pull away but instead should push *toward* our assailant. This provided the element of surprise. Then, once we'd surprised, we should use any means—teeth, claws, car keys, whatever—to inflict maximum pain.

So I went *toward* Manuel and used my teeth on the side of his gripping hand. I used them so hard that I felt his flesh break beneath them. I also, of course, heard him howl.

And Miss Barr was right: he did let go. I ran through the mud, my feet sliding this way and that, Manuel's stentorian Spanish curses way too close behind me.

His hand closed on my shoulder and he spun me around with a strength I'd never dreamed he had. I stared at the contortion that was his face. "Why you hurt me?" he whined, his eyes brimming with tears. "Why, señora, why?" He raised his injured hand, though not to strike me. Instead he sucked at the blood that was oozing through the wound I'd just inflicted.

I backed away. "Stay away from me, Manuel," I yelled.

He dropped to his knees as if to pray. He raised his face to the pelting rain and shouted again, "Ayeeee."

His eyes were closed. I think there were tears easing out from under his lids.

Well, they say that women get hurt because we're pushovers. We don't really want to put our all into pummeling the assailant, so we hold back, and as a result, the assailant wins. So I thought how I should lay a karate chop along Manuel's Adam's apple while I had the chance, but guess what?

I couldn't.

I mean, the guy looked so pathetic down there on his knees. And by this time I could see that he was bawling. He had lost the battle with the blood, too. His hand was black with it in the rain.

"Why you do this to me, señora?" he whimpered.

My femininity won out over my feminism. I knelt beside him, mud and all. I cupped his hand in mine, and I winced when he winced at my touch. "Manuel," I said. "Come to the house. I'll put something on this for you."

Like most bleeding wounds, once the gush had stopped and the thing was all cleaned up, it didn't look like as horrible as expected. Still, I wasn't all that eager to explain what I had done to the local emergency-room staff, either.

Fortunately, Manuel refused to go there.

And fortunately, too, he hadn't arrived at our farm in order to kill me. Instead, he told me, he'd come because he had information to convey. To me, because I, out of all the gringos and gringas he'd encountered, had treated him the best.

I smiled crookedly when he said this. I hoped there wasn't any residual blood from his hand on my fangs.

But first things first. We had to find Plum and put her up for the night. With that in mind, I scooped some grain into a pail, grabbed a flashlight, and prepared to go out once again into the muddy night.

"I go, too," Manuel said.

The rain had stopped, but the ground was totally soaked. We could hear the squish as we walked. This is very unusual for Texas.

I rattled the grain against the edges of the pail. "Come on, girl," I sang. "Come on."

We listened for some sign of her, soft blowing or the fall of a hoof, but there was nothing.

"Find footprint," Manuel advised, taking the light away and casting it on the ground. Sure enough, even with all the rain, there were deep horse tracks that we could follow.

Not very much later, Plum succumbed to the greed so fortunately inherent in the equine species. Thus we were able to capture her and lead her home.

Watching Manuel stroke her neck and watching Plum grooving on the strokes made me feel especially foolish for the assumption I'd made about Manuel, even if it had been fleeting. Manuel batted all of my apologies aside, saying no, no, that he'd frightened me. The bite had been his own fault.

I kept wondering what he'd feel tomorrow when his wound began to throb as wounds will do the second day. I wondered what had become of the painkillers that the dentist had given Jeet. They were codeine, I thought. Which, technically speaking, would make me a narcotics trafficker on top of everything else. I decided to confine my sympathies to speech and hope that Manuel didn't have a Spanish-speaking lawyer friend to whom he might, *in extremis*, turn.

Meanwhile, Manuel told me his tale, how he'd eavesdropped in the barn and heard Vince say that a horse had accidentally killed Nika. How he'd known from my response that I hadn't believed it. How he knew, as I did, that it wasn't true.

He'd tried to call me on the phone, he said, even before he'd heard me say that, but he'd chickened out when my recording came on. He'd had to tell someone what he knew.

Manuel had a natural talent for suspense. Because so far all of this was prelude. About what he knew, his big info lode, I still hadn't a clue.

Finally he got around to the crucial stuff. "Someone kill Señora Ballinger," he said. "Someone."

"What do you mean, Manuel?" I urged. "Who?"

By this time we were back in the kitchen and I'd persuaded Manuel to soak his hand in a bowl of cool water. It was starting to swell, but he didn't seem to notice. While I was patting it dry, however, he trembled whenever the towel came near.

He'd probably need rabies shots or something.

Meanwhile, he continued with his story.

He'd been sent away on an errand by Nika that morning. A fool's errand, he called it. "The kind where I know she don't want me around," he explained.

He'd finished early, though, and he'd come back to find Señora Ballinger near death. "Her face," he summarized. "And the blood."

I'd only heard about it on TV, but still, I shuddered along with him.

He went through pretty much what I already knew. But then he added the part that had fueled his suspicion: the video camera that Nika always used to record her lessons was gone, tripod and all. "I look ever-where," he said. So he was sure it had been stolen. It had been there at the barn that morning. It had been there since Nika first bought it.

What was more, the week before, he'd spied to see why Nika had been sending him away. He'd sneaked back to Cliffside Farm and . . .

I felt the juicy part was nigh. I caught my breath. And Manuel, Hitchcockian that he was proving to be, paused maddeningly. "Señora," he said, gesturing at the wound. "You have basset . . . basset . . . ?"

"Bacitracin, right!" What horse owner is ever without it? I rushed to get it, wondering what Manuel had in store. Who might Nika have been tupping? The blacksmith? The UPS man? Who?

Manuel dabbed the Bacitracin on his hand. Wrapped his handkerchief around it. Sighed.

"Manuel," I said.

"It was a woman, Her-man you would say."

"A woman named Herman?"

Manuel actually laughed. "No, señora, from Hermany, how you say, Alemania."

"Germany, I get it."

"Frau Katerina was her name," he said.

Oh, right. Katerina Schwetman, no doubt. Mother of Germany's primo dressage riders, twins named Thea and Nan. And Katerina was once pretty primo herself, with three individual Olympic golds, no less.

Not that international hotshots don't come here to teach us, mind. That's practically how they support themselves, in fact. It's just that I couldn't imagine someone as stellar as Frau Katerina Schwetman coming here to give a rider of Nika's ilk a private session no matter what Nika had been willing to pay.

But "Frau Katerina give lessons to Señora Ballinger," Manuel insisted.

"Who told you that?" I asked.

"I heard. I saw."

But he had to be wrong. If someone like that had

that you didn't. Suzie stuck it in your mailbox. For God's sake, Robin, go and look." She slammed the phone down in my ear.

I tried to call her back, but the line was busy. So I put my dirty clothes back on and slogged through the mud in the driveway all the way down to the mailbox. And guess what? Suzie hadn't stuck anything of the sort in there. The mailbox was as bare as Mother Hubbard's cupboard.

So I slogged back up the driveway and called Lola. "I have just been to the mailbox," I fumed. "I repeat: *What flier?*"

"Oh," Lo says. "I'll find out what happened."

"Wait a minute," I yelled. I could tell she was about to hang up again. "What's this all about?"

"The horse," Lo said. "Suzie figured out who the horse was. The horse in Nika's picture."

"Well, who is it?"

"Let me go find Suzie, okay?" And she was gone.

I went upstairs to my sanctuary. Most of the bubbles on the foot end of the tub remained. On the head end, the bubbles were gone and the water they'd departed to reveal was a kind of yucky gray. It was the same with the candles. One had fizzled out altogether, another, a tall one, listed way to the left, but the others still shone. The station was into a commercial break, however. I spun the dial and settled for some U-2. I glugged the wine down, then slid into the tepid gray depths, thinking, without wanting to, of the scene in *The Year of Living Dangerously* where the guy dives into the algae-covered swimming pool.

And the phone rang yet again.

"Okay," Lola said, "here's the deal. It's a clinic in Houston tomorrow, Friday, and Saturday. At Braedock. And it's—get this—Katerina Schwetman."

"But you said the horse," I protested.

"Right. There's a picture of Katerina Schwetman on one of her horses, Spier, and he's the one."

"Oh, right. Nika riding one of Katerina Schwetman's finest. Give me a break."

"Robin, come over here and see for yourself if you don't believe me."

I considered this, but given my half-bathed, wine-filled state, decided not to. "I'll come tomorrow. And I do believe you. Tell me what the number at Braedock is." I wrote it down.

I considered. Could Lola and Manuel both be wrong? I doubted it. And both had tied this Nika thing to Frau Katerina Schwetman. But that seemed utterly bizarre.

Frau Schwetman had been quoted more than once in various horse magazines as having made really snotty remarks about Americans and America's chances in world-class dressage. As a matter of fact, on the one occasion when an American rider did win the World Cup, Frau Schwetman had called it a fluke. In the interview she had laughed about the fact that the awards ceremony had to be delayed because the orchestra didn't have the music for "The Star Spangled Banner" and the World Cup management didn't have an American flag on hand because no one in their wildest dreams had ever imagined an American would win.

Well, okay, that was true, but did she have to rub our noses in it? All the other biggies had congratulated us on the win.

Of course, that's exactly why everyone over here would *want* to study with the woman, probably. It's like we're major toads in this regard. We pay these clinicians from Europe. (We call them clinicians because we don't want to admit that we're hiring them to be instructors. See, we don't go to lessons, we ride in clinics instead. Never mind that an hour in a clinic is a lesson, we pretend that there's an enormous difference.) Anyway, we pay these clinicians who are name riders or trainers or coaches in Europe to come over here and tell us exactly how bad we are, and how bad our horses are, too. If we chance to get one who tells us something *good*, we decide he's too lenient. So of course we would want the imperious Frau Katerina to do us in.

You think I'm kidding, don't you? Except that I went to one clinic where everyone came out of the arena crying. Not only that, but all day long I'd find people crying everywhere. Crying at the snack bar, crying in the john. And *this* clinic was conducted by someone that our local dressage club keeps trying to have come back. That's right, come *back*. Except—can you guess? The guy is booked solid. Booked on through the next thirty years.

It's like Lola once said: Dressage, pure dressage, exists to satisfy our masochistic needs.

But would Frau Schwetman really want to teach Nika?

I mean, I could see her offering to coach someone really good, like Melissa Song, but Nika? I ran this by Lola, but Lo was cynical.

"People will do anything for money," she said. "And face it, Nika had money up the wazoo. Besides, you know these coaches are over here all the time. They'll teach anybody who can pay for it."

"But a private lesson! It makes you want to puke."

I was reacting to the way Nika had ridden more than anything else. I mean, you only had to watch her once to know there was no hope there.

When there is hope—I mean when a rider evinces some special talent—it isn't unusual for a master from another country to offer to help. Oh sure, there's money involved, but sappy as it sounds, there's also the pure love of the sport.

Did Katerina Schwetman have any of that? Could she, and at the same time try to teach Nika?

But Lola was ready to burst my bubble there, too. "Most of us are Nikas," she said. "It's just a matter of degree."

That smarted just a bit, which had been Lo's intention.

I called Braedock, which is the name Edith Conover and her big-time criminal lawyer husband, Harry "Greenback" Conover, have given their place. And the next thing I know I am stammering into Edith's ear, "T-t-two hundred dollars?"

"It sounds high, I know," Edith Conover is saying, "but she's a three-time Olympic gold medal winner. And her twins, both of them, are—"

"I know," I say, "I know."

"But this is all very much beside the point because we simply have no slots. The clinic has been full since we announced it. We sent the flier around to get auditors and, well"—here Edith chuckles merrily—"perhaps to boast a bit. About having someone of Frau Schwetman's caliber here at all."

"Yeah, well, how did that happen anyway?" I asked.

"You'll probably think I'm making this up"—Edie laughed—"but the fact is, Katerina Schwetman called *me*. She asked me all about Braedock—how close it was to downtown Houston and all of that and then, *mirabile dictu*, she suggested offering a clinic!"

How many people do you know who can inject an expression like *mirabile dictu* into a simple conversation? I'm just wondering, because I seem to know several. It defies the national average, I bet.

"She was just in the neighborhood," I asked, "or what?"

"Nothing that casual," Edith said. "Well, that's what I assume. Because she even offered to bring her own horse in for demos, a stallion, and I couldn't believe that she'd gotten him through quarantine and all that."

Quarantine takes a while. "So she planned this trip," I ventured.

"Definitely."

"And there was no publicity."

"Just what we put out. Fliers. No national publicity, no. As far as I know, this is the only clinic she's offering."

I took a deep breath. "Was Veronika Ballinger supposed to ride?" I asked.

There was a painful pause, then a stiff reply. "Even if Veronika had been scheduled to ride, her slot would have gone to the first name on our waiting list."

"Oh, I didn't mean it that way. I didn't mean that I wanted her slot." What did she think I was, a ghoul?

She sounded relieved. "Well, actually, you wouldn't be the first person to ask for it. Ever since Veronika's death we've had many very hopeful calls. But frankly, Veronika never held a slot. I don't understand it, really. She was one of the first people I contacted and initially she seemed quite eager."

"Oh, really."

"Yes. Originally Veronika said I could probably put her down for two rides a day, every day, but then a couple of days later she called back and said never mind."

Because she'd arranged to get Frau Schwetman to come to Cliffside early for some private lessons, I realized. "That is weird," I said. Then I had a brainstorm.

"Look," I said, "I'm obviously not going to get into

this clinic, but how about if I come to groom? Wouldn't someone need an extra groom? I've done it before," I added, "a lot." Once for Lola, but never mind.

"Oh!" Edith brightened. "Well, *do* come, yes. In fact, if you want to bring a horse down just in case . . ."

That was going to be my next question, since I couldn't very well leave Plum behind with Jeet gone and Lola still mad at me.

"You might get lucky," Edith said. "And if someone pulls a shoe or can't ride for some reason, you just might . . ."

"Be able to fill in!" I said, adding silently, For a mere two hundred dollars an hour. Right.

I consoled myself with the knowledge that (a) Jeet was out of town and (b) chances of actually having to part with two hundred big ones were minimal. But if by some queer quirk of fate this turned out to happen, it meant that I'd have to add writing a bad check on my depleted farm account to my growing list of criminal misdeeds.

Maybe I could hire Edith Conover's husband.

I had just decided to blow out my candles, pull the plug on my Vitabath, and start packing when the phone rang yet again.

"For someone who's mad at me," I told Lo, "you sure do call a lot."

"Shut up and listen," Lola said. "There's something else. I had to go rooting around in Suzie's tack trunk for this flier and I found another picture."

"Jeez. It's like *Blow-Up*, equine style," I cracked.

Lo evidently hadn't seen *Blow-Up*. "I wasn't going to say anything, but I can't help it, this is too juicy. Robin, it's a picture of Suzie and someone who looks an awful lot like Ron cavorting on a beach someplace."

"The plot thickens. Listen, I'll come over right away."

"No, it's too late now," Lola stalled. "Anyway, you said tomorrow."

"But now I'm going to Houst—"

"Tomorrow's fine," Lo allowed, before hanging up on me yet again.

I felt like going over there anyway just to see why I couldn't. But then I realized that either I was just being childish and that Lola had every right to change her mind or else it was sinister and that Lola all of a sudden was trying to hide something from me. Except, if the latter, why would she have told me about the picture of Suzie and Ron?

Deep in my heart I am probably not a very nice person. I know this because I immediately called Vince to gloat about the recent evidence indicating that he and the stupid police were wrong. Vince wasn't at home, but I managed to unload onto his recorder. I mentioned that there was crucial data of a suspicious nature. Because I didn't quite know what the Frau Schwetman information meant and her name wouldn't mean diddly to a non-horse person, I refrained from mentioning it. Despite not having seen it, I was way more elaborate about the photo of Ron and Suz.

Needless to add, I was so atwitter at this point that I couldn't sleep. Every time I shut my eyes and started to drift off, I'd get that atavistic feeling that I was falling. Atavistic because it's supposed to derive from our ape days, when we slept in trees.

Well, my mind now made the obvious leap from ape to Ron, and before I knew it, I was unhitching the trailer, thinking I'd just cruise by Ron's office, pay a midnight call. Okay, I had a hunch.

CHAPTER 9

Ron's headquarters were smack downtown, in an historical building that had been all spiffed up. So, dark as it was, I knew what I was looking at: high chic, high ceilings, high rent.

I stood at the entrance and ran my hand over the mortar that had been used to place the red bricks. Then I touched the heavy, painted woodwork trim. I must have looked like some undercover building inspector.

I looked down at the mosaic tiles that composed the entry floor. The name of the building had been tiled in there and I read what it said. It was the date, 1859, which in Texas is old. And there was a name, too. I finally made it out: ALBRIGHT BUILDING.

Albright. As in Lola?

But I couldn't follow this train of thought, because just then, I became aware of a hulking form just behind me. Immediately—before I could react—the hulk reached his arms around me. Both of them.

One hairy forearm was smashed up against my face. The other arm encircled my waist. It felt as though one squeeze from either would do me in.

I was trying to come up with a reaction, but the one that had served me so well with Manuel—biting—was out of the question because my mouth wouldn't move.

Then the lights inside the building flared on.

Great, I thought. Whoever it is has got an accomplice.

Whoever it was began to whisper, "Robin. Promise me you won't make a sound. I'm going to ease up on you now, but you have to promise not to make a sound or a move of any kind. Okay?"

I nodded as much as I could nod under the circumstances. And whoever it was eased up.

But I had lied. As soon as I could get my mouth free, I closed it down on whoever-it-was's arm, and as I shoved back against him and ran toward my truck, I had the satisfaction of hearing him howl the way Manuel had, like a banshee.

By the time I reached the truck, the front door to the building had opened and Ron had lumbered outside. I had been wrong about him being the other guy's accomplice. In fact, he began to beat up on the man who had grabbed me.

That man turned out to be Vince.

Every so often I could hear a few of Ron's words. His favorite seemed to be "effing" but I also picked up on "reporters" and "snoops" and "middle of the night." These were punctuated by the sound of Ron's fist connecting with Vince's bone. Jawbone. Cheekbone. Nose. Occasionally there was the muffled sound of fist hitting tummy.

I didn't know what to do. True, Vince had grabbed me, but I couldn't stand seeing him getting hit like this, over and over again. On the other hand, what's to say Ron wouldn't do the same to me, like round two?

I had to stop this. I started Mother, aimed at the fray, and gunned her.

Well, Ron did drop Vince, of course. He ran back inside, and then he slammed and bolted the door. I caught Vince in Mother's headlights and went running to where he lay.

He was a mess, bloody nose, torn earlobe, already blackened eye. There was blood all over the ground, all over his clothes. And it was still coming from all those places in thick, red streams.

I ran back to the truck and grabbed up whatever I thought would help: leg wraps and saddle pads and half a jar of year-old Gatorade.

After cradling Vince's head in my arms and swabbing his injuries with Gatorade (which evidently stings, by the way), I ascertained that despite their horrific appearance, none of the wounds beneath the gore was life threatening. Therefore I spoke. "I'll tell you what, Vincent," I said. "I'll drive you over to the police station. You can formally complain that Ron assaulted you and then I'll formally complain about the way you assaulted me."

Vince groaned. "I can't talk," he said. "It hurts too much."

I had a stab of fear: broken ribs. My voice lost its razor edge. "I'll drive you to the hospital first, though," I told him.

He propped himself up on his elbows. "I don't want to go to the hospital," he said. "I'm okay. He just knocked the breath out of me."

I was planning to argue, but Ron put a stop to that. He was suddenly hovering over us like some huge human condor bent on carrying us away to his lair. Sure enough, "Inside," he said.

I helped Vince to his feet and we hobbled on ahead of Ron. I couldn't help wondering why this part of the city's streets was so infrequently traveled, but of course Ron was right, it *was* by now the middle of the night and this was, more or less, a business district. Still, you'd think the police would be out cruising around, wouldn't you?

Anyway, we entered the building. We sat in the seats Ron indicated, old-timey plush velvet chairs meant for visitors who were cooling their heels. I noted with some satisfaction that Vince was oozing fresh red blood onto the backrest of his. Proof, I thought. Or at the least a reupholstering bill.

It was a gorgeous place, tall and seemingly ancient brick walls, wide-planked floor, heavy brass hardware. The kind of place you'd expect to find in the New Orleans French Quarter. And it was tasteful, too; not at all the sort of office you'd expect a lug like Ron Ballinger to have. He, evidently, like his departed wife, Nika, had his own store of surprises.

From deep in the back somewhere, I heard someone pounding on thick wood. Ron yelled that the door was open, and two very young police officers waltzed into the room.

"It's okay," Ron said to them. "Turns out I know these two. They just wanted to have a little chat."

"Hey, wait a minute," I squealed, and pointed at Vince, "He beat the crap out of my friend here. I'm a witness."

The police looked over at Vince, who was smiling weakly though still seeping blood, then back at Ron.

Ron spoke to the cops. "Like I told you on the phone, he was trying to break in."

And Vince said, "Not exactly true, but I can see where he might have thought that."

Despite the seepage, Vince was starting to look pretty healthy. He smelled like Gatorade, though. I kept imagining the fire ants that are everywhere in Texas nudging each other down under the concrete of the city streets and preparing to make a Cecil B. deMille march toward Vince's sticky-sweet person.

"I'd like a police escort out of here," I said.

The police looked to Ron.

Ron shrugged indulgently. "Far as I'm concerned, they can both go with you, but I need to visit with both of them for a minute first."

Visit, right. He was probably going to resume beating Vince where he'd left off.

"We'll be right outside," one of the cops said. And then they actually *left*.

Ron turned to us and dropped his voice into the hiss range so that the cops outside couldn't possibly hear. "Stay away from me and stay away from my house and my office, or next time I'll have you both tossed in the crapper, you hear?"

Vince glared at him and he glared at Vince and I glared at Vince, too, just before I turned back to glare at Ron. "What about your relationship with Suzie?" I asked Ron.

"Suzie? What are you, dense? You never heard of an extramarital affair? And now," he reminded me, "it isn't *even* extra. Jesus. What are you, some kind of religious nut or what?"

I had to admit, this had the ring of truth. An ugly truth, but that didn't exactly matter. "And what about this building?" I tried.

"This building? I own it, that's what. It's private property and I want you off."

With that he huffed to the door and flung it wide. Vince and I sort of looked at each other apologetically and then began slouching in that direction.

Vince and I agreed to meet at Katz's, an all-night establishment on Sixth Street, and he went toward his car to drive there. Under the watchful eye of Austin's finest, I headed toward my own vehicle. Mysteriously, it was no longer in the center of the street where I had left it, but was pulled to the curb. Nor were its headlights on.

"Thanks, guys," I told the cops.

They exchanged sheepish looks and I knew right then the reason. Sure enough, there was a ticket affixed to my windshield.

"I was aiding an injured person," I whined.

"If you say that in court, you'll beat it," one of the cops advised.

"In court? Can't you just tear it up?" I had to lift myself halfway up onto the hood just in order to reach the ticket.

"Sorry. Once we've written it . . ." one began.

"But if you tell the judge what you were doing . . ." the other offered.

Gallantly, they watched me drive away.

The fact that Vince had ordered potato pancakes for me helped, but only slightly. "Why'd you grab me?" I wanted to know.

"I knew that he was inside," he said. "I was there when he arrived. And there you were, plowing right up toward the door."

"Oh," I said. "Well, how come you were there at all? You're the one who said Nika's death was an accident."

"I was there because you called me. And anyway, all I said was that the *police* thought it was an accident."

I tried to remember if that, indeed, was what he'd said.

He went on. "To be honest, Robin, I didn't want to have to contend with you. I mean, I didn't need you snooping around."

"Snooping around!"

He narrowed his eyes in a Jeet-like manner and I knew my indignation was for naught.

"Robin," he said. "I really want to get out of the newspaper business. I want to write a book. A true crime. This was going to be my baby, and I didn't want you around mucking things up.''

My pancakes had arrived, so I let this pass.

''And,'' he rolled on, ''I sure as hell knew that Jeet wouldn't want you getting mixed up in this.''

I held my tongue. I asked for sour cream and apple-sauce and waited until the waiter brought it. ''So the police *are* investigating,'' I said after a while.

''For sure.''

''Ron?''

''Maybe.''

''Suz?''

''Could be.''

''How about Manuel?'' I tried.

''Probably.''

''In other words,'' I translated, ''the police are ab-solutely everywhere and nowhere. The only thing they know for sure is that it *wasn't* an accident.''

''No,'' Vince said, ''they don't know that either. Not for sure.''

I tuned him out, focusing instead on the grub. Vince may not be fun to talk to, but he's fun to observe. For instance, he would roll his eyes before every mouthful of his migas, which, if you aren't from this region, is an egg dish that includes in its scramble a lovely mix of tortilla bits and peppers and cheese and such.

I waited until he was all done and then I asked if he had neglected to tell me anything.

''About what?'' he said.

CHAPTER 10

To put it mildly, I was not in any condition to be transporting horses on our nation's highways. But in this early stage of sleep deprivation, I was hyperalert. I have no doubt that I looked semicrazed—which I frequently do when I'm pulling a horse trailer anyway. Such responsibility! And I don't have to tell you about all of the nuts who are driving around out there.

I had pretty much left Austin right after I got in from Katz's, figuring I would stop first at the address that Manuel had given me for Nika's mom. I had a Houston map, and it looked as though the address was right at a cloverleaf of the interstate itself. This was peculiar enough to arouse my suspicions. What? Was she born in a warehouse instead of a nice mid-to-upper-class neighborhood like the rest of us?

I hadn't told Vince about the mother angle, nor had I mentioned the Frau Schwetman thing, of course. If he could be cagey with me, I'd be cagey right back. And anyway, I didn't want to hear him telling me my plans were stupid even while they were still just plans. Men, I have discovered, have a tendency to do this.

But back to the address and its curious location: I now pictured some glass-and-concrete high rise where Nika had been mailing laundered drug money or something. What do they call it in movies? A drop.

And having a horse with me pretty much would render me, maybe not inconspicuous, but certainly beyond suspicion. I mean, what self-respecting detective would go snooping around while transporting a horse?

So whatever anyone might have thought of my plans had I divulged them, I felt pretty good. Plus, Plum was being quiet back there—very important to my state of mental well-being.

Believe me, a horse's every move can be felt by the person who is pulling the trailer. Kind of the way a horse can feel a rider's every move. An opportunity for revenge, I've sometimes suspected, usually while careening from one side of a narrow highway to another, propelled by the thrashing and pawing of an animal who isn't happy back there. I know, it sounds impossible— I mean, a trailer is a separate entity connected only by a metal hitch and a couple of chains and electric wires— but take my word for it. Or if you don't want to take my word, ask around. Anyone who's ever pulled a horse trailer can tell you. Horror stories abound.

As I neared my geographical goal another point about trailering came to mind. It takes a long, heavy truck-and-trailer combo a helluva lot of time to stop. And turns must be preplanned, too. All of this became important as I tried to find the address of Nika's mom.

On the map it seemed right smack at the juncture. In real life, there was no juncture, just an endless looping of concrete span. I looped and looped and looped again, thinking that Plum would probably qualify to go up in the space shuttle after all of this. Finally I took an exit and, by asking various street urchins, found myself there.

No glass high rise. Nothing even resembling respectability. Maybe, I thought, Manuel had written the address down wrong.

Because I was parked in front of a wan little house in the shadow of the interstate ramps.

I mean wan. And I mean little. It was one of those peeling-shingle jobs enclosed in a Cyclone fence, the kind of house that looks as if it contains about four hundred square feet total.

And this was a particularly shabby specimen, the shingles hanging half off along the whole right side. The house was up on cement blocks, too, exposing a trash-strewn expanse of barren ground.

The parts of the yard that weren't overgrown were devoid of vegetation, too.

Nika's mother? No way, I thought. Still, I got out of the truck and walked back to check on my horse. I opened the side window and there Plum was, drowsing, her snout pressed against the hay net.

"Lady, can I pet him?" a little voice asked.

I looked down and saw a round-faced Mexican boy about eight or nine.

Plum awakened and thrust her nose through the window. I could see her thinking, Possible carrot here.

But of course she was high off the ground, far too high for the urchin to pet. I tried to give the kid a boost, and he did manage a little nose pat.

Plum expelled some air and a spray of spittle. Her way of protesting the child's lack of a treat.

"You want something, lady?" A man about my height had pulled the child from my grasp and was staring me down.

"Uh, I'm looking for . . ." I paused, trying to remember the name that Manuel had written down above the address. "Señora Ballinger's mother," I tried.

"Oh, *sí*." The man brightened. "In there." He

pointed at the selfsame wan little house. "She talk about her daughter all the time."

"Wanna pet, wanna pet the horsie," the cherubic little boy began to chant.

"Go ahead," I said, responding to the question in the man's eye. He had obviously removed me from his list of potential kidnappers and child molesters. "Pet all you want. Watch out that she doesn't nip your fingers, though."

Plum can do that if she thinks you're holding out on her.

I got a couple carrots out of the cooler on my front seat. "Here," I said, breaking one into four pieces and handing them to the child.

At the sound of the snap, Plum went into Orange Alert, ears pricked, a dozen notches more alive than she'd been seconds ago.

Nika's mother—there was no mistaking the resemblance—wore a housedress from the forties, I swear. She had bedroom slippers on her feet, and her hair was up in big fat rollers. She yawned hello.

"I'm a friend of Nika's," I said.

She was blank.

"Your daughter."

"Ronnie," she said.

"Veronika," I acknowledged.

She stepped aside and I slipped past her, though with some reluctance. "I, uh"—I gestured toward the street—"have my horse with me."

She nodded yes as if to ask, *What else is new?*

Back to the resemblance. It was odd because this was the low-income version of Nika, older and more wrinkled, of course, but more than that. Sallow-skinned, wizened not so much by age but by, probably, a horrible diet. With teeth that seemed not to have ever visited a dentist, much less an orthodontist. She was Nika without advantages.

"I'm sorry about your daughter," I said. I had no idea whether or not she even knew that Nika was dead. I steeled myself, hoping I wouldn't have to tell her.

She lowered her eyes, then raised them again. She knew. "She done real good, though, my Ronnie," she said.

"Real good," I seconded.

Nika's mother sighed. Then she took me into what I can only describe as the shrine: a hallway completely papered with memorabilia, clippings about Nika, yellowed photographs thumbtacked right to the wall.

"I take the Austin paper," she explained.

There were even photocopies of Nika's dressage tests—I kid you not! "Did she send you these?" I asked, incredulous.

"Nearly ever' week," the woman said.

Jeez. You'd think that maybe she could have sent her mother money or something. But no. She sent her tests. I looked at some of her scores. The highest one was forty-nine.

"She rides real good," her mom went on. "She would have made the Olympics. Here, look." She took a velvet box out of a drawer, and sure enough, there, but huge and in color, was the photograph of Nika in the top hat and shadbelly coat. The picture that had made me curious in the first place.

"Is this her horse?" I asked. Of course I already knew. So disembowel me, already.

"Naw. Belongs to this coach of hers. Can't rightly recall the name, but no, it wasn't hers."

Nika going to the Olympics, right. And I'll be addressing the United Nations tomorrow morning. Right after breakfast with H. Ross Perot. A light breakfast. I mean, I had to sing at the Met, then dance *Swan Lake* an hour later.

I'd have remembered her if she'd have been up front at Nika's funeral or later on at Ron's. "You didn't come to Austin for the"—I tried, but I couldn't make my mouth say funeral—"uh, services."

"She wouldn't have wanted me to," Nika's mother said. "She always wanted me to stay out of things. Out of her life, kind of. I guess she was ashamed of me."

My face reddened. I felt the heat.

"It's all right," the woman assured me. "I don't blame her, in a way. She was on a different level, you might say. Always trying to raise me up, too. Wanted me to move out of here. To a trailer park, maybe, a really nice one with maybe a birdbath in the yard or something. But I said no, I kind of like it here."

She asked if I wanted to see Nika's room, and I did. It was off the bathroom, what you might call a walk-in closet. There was a cot in there, one of those canvas army jobs that's more or less like a hammock up on stilts.

I flashed back to the room in Nika's house. Of course. She was creating the childhood room she'd never had.

"This is it," Nika's mother said. "Where Ronnie grew up. She always knew what she wanted and she got it, too. Money, horses, cars. She picked Ron Ballinger out of a newspaper story and then she went up there to Austin and married him."

"She what? What do you mean?"

"Here." She produced a page from an old newspaper citing the fifty richest men in Texas. Ron was one of several whose name had been circled.

"He was the first one she went after, too. Got him

right out of the chute. She was only seventeen when he married her.''

I was more than incredulous, I was kind of lost in admiration. Nika hadn't been idly rich all her life. Her life, as she'd presented her past to us—degree in classical archaeology and all—had been completely made up. She'd invented the past and then she'd engineered the future, no mean feat.

"I always knew those horses of hers would kill her, though," Nika's mother said.

"What do you mean?" I asked. It was beginning to sound like my mantra.

"They're big, they're mean. It seemed like it just had to happen one of these days, is all."

"You think one of the horses killed your daughter," I said.

"That's the way Mr. Ballinger's secretary told it to me when she called to say my Ronnie had passed and how they took care of the funeral and all."

Ron, the bum, hadn't even bothered to call her himself. And lest she show up and embarrass anybody, they'd called her after the fact.

"She done real good." Nika's mother seemed to be talking to God now rather than to me. Her eyes were uplifted. "She dropped outta high school in tenth grade and then she went on to the Geneva Wheeler Modeling School. My Ronnie, she made something out of herself."

I don't know how I felt as I drove on to Braedock and the clinic. I was weary, but it wasn't only physical, brought on by the drive and the fact that I hadn't had any sleep the night before. It was as though the weariness inherent in Nika's home, Nika's past, Nika's mother, had begun to weigh me down. I could imagine

Nika as a little girl, always aspiring to more than what she had. Nika dreaming the way all kids dream, but in Nika's case, actually pulling it off.

Me, I'd come from better—or maybe I should say more privileged circumstances—and here I was, driving up to a mansion not too terribly unlike the one that Nika had scored for herself. And what was I? A lowly groom.

<u>CHAPTER</u> 11

Did I say mansion? Well, yes, but mansion is a house, one house. Braedock was a vast estate that included a huge manor house and—well, forgive me for sounding like an advertising person in a slump—but much, much more.

How can I best describe it? Let me see. Did you see the film *Rebecca*? Do you remember the part where Laurence Olivier is taking Joan Fontaine to his ancestral home? They drive through these massive wrought-iron gates and up a long, tree-lined driveway, and suddenly there's a break in the trees and there it is:

MANDERLAY

Okay, so now substitute the name Braedock, and you've got the picture.

Let's talk about the mansion first. It's three stories tall with maybe eight chimneys looming over the vast expanse of slate roof. The word *mansard* occurs to me, but I don't really know why. It probably has to do with some course I took in college.

There must be twenty rooms in this place judging from all of the windows. You just know there's a library and a morning room and probably a ballroom, too.

Scratch what I'd been saying about Nika and all that

she had scored. Because Braedock made Ron and Nika's Cliffside look low rent.

Like, though you can *see* the mansion, before you actually get right up to it, the road forks. A sign indicates that the stables are off to the left.

And my God, the stables!

They look almost as good as the manse, except that they're a single story tall. But the doors are arched, thick oak with great big wrought-iron hinges, and the walls are old brick edged with stone.

The indoor arena is the same kind of architecture. It's recognizable as an arena, though, because despite cosmetic attempts to make it match the rest, it is still an expanse the size and span of an airplane hangar.

I'm trying to figure out where to go with my rig when a woman comes out of what looks like an addition to the arena and waves at me. She's saying something, but I'm unable to hear.

She comes running up to the truck. "Robin?" she asks.

I tell her yes.

"I'm Edie Conover," she says. "You can unload here. I'll show you where to put your stuff."

The stall is so clean that I feel as though I'll die of embarrassment the minute Plum poops in it. Which, of course, is as soon as she enters and stops snorting.

But out of nowhere a man appears, muckrake and basket in hand.

"I thought I . . ." I begin, thinking, Well, hell, if I'm a groom, maybe I should be raking it up and not the Braedock staff.

Edie reads what I'm thinking and laughs. "No," she says, "you don't have to do stalls. If you'll just take the horses after each person's ride and get their tack off and hose them down, maybe walk them. Someone else will clean the tack off, too. In most cases, anyway.''

"You mean I'll be able to watch most of the sessions?'' I'm incredulous.

"Sure. And before you ask me, no, you don't have to pay the auditor's fee either.'' Word of my pinchpenny status must have spread.

Jeez, I hadn't even considered what the auditor's fee might be.

"Is she . . . ?'' I began, about to ask about Frau Schwetman, whether she'd arrived.

"She's here. She's up at the house, resting.''

I don't know why, but I thought of Count Dracula in his coffin gathering energy for the upcoming nocturnal blood quest.

"What's she like?'' I asked.

"Well, it's odd,'' Edie answered. "She looks very sweet, but she's very forceful, very Germanic.''

When I actually saw her in the flesh, I knew what Edie meant. Because the great Katerina was small, maybe five-two or three and round-faced, with twinkly blue eyes and tweakable cheeks. Her hair was gunmetal gray. It had been braided and wrapped around her scalp in a matronly way. She looked as though she ought to be in some big old-fashioned kitchen mashing potatoes and maybe stuffing a goose.

Of course the woman's appearance had to be deceiving. You don't *charm* a half ton of horseflesh around a dressage arena, after all. So Frau Katerina Schwetman could probably crack walnuts with her thighs.

She was spreading those thighs even as I observed her for the first time. She was, in fact, about to ride Edie Conover's big chestnut Oldenburg gelding in a pre-clinic introductory display. The clinic proper would be-

gin immediately afterward, when each of the eight
participants would get a forty-five-minute private session. That was when I would be called upon to fetch
and carry.

Some of the riders had brought grooms of their very
own. Edie explained that I'd still be the one to take the
horses away. Except for one untouchable, who was
owned by Elsbeth something or other, two names with
a hyphen. That would mean that I had a relatively easy
job, while the real grooms would be doing the not-so-
pleasant things like swabbing off the sweat-drenched
saddles and wiping away the slobber-covered bits and
bridles.

Not bad.

By this time Frau Schwetman had finished adjusting
her stirrup leathers to suit her own relatively short and
decidedly chunky legs. I wondered what she'd had to
face as a rider in Germany, where almost all the riders
seem to have legs so long they could knot them at the
ankle under the horse's belly. In pictures they look like
this, anyway. And of course there was nothing anorexic
about the old dame either.

Everyone up to this point had been chattering. As
Frau Schwetman picked up the reins the talking, but for
an occasional whisper, stopped. From then on in, however, we all watched in reverent silence.

No exaggeration.

For me it was like seeing the burning bush.

Because in minutes the horse was trotting with an
energy that seemed total, complete. He kind of arced
his neck onto the bit, and you could almost see the
impulsion traveling like a visible band that moved
through Frau Schwetman's legs to the horse's hindquarters, through Frau Schwetman's arms into the horse's
mouth.

"So this is what dressage really looks like," I said, instantly regretting how stupid that must have sounded.

"I was thinking the exact same thing," Edie said.

"But he's your horse," I protested.

"I've never been able to get him to look this way," Edie said. "Believe me, I never even knew he *could*."

I've read bunches of books about dressage, about the way the horse ought to look, even one that defined dressage as "calling forth the horse's beauty." This was the first time I'd seen it for real.

It was like—well, like the Georges Rouault painting *The Old King*. My parents had a print of it, and my elementary school had a print of it, and I thought I knew what the painting looked like. Then I was in a museum and I found myself in the presence of the original. The original. It was the print intensified a hundredfold. I had never seen color so deep, or brushstrokes so certain.

Well, seeing Katerina Schwetman ride was just like seeing that Rouault. I'm not kidding. You wouldn't need a degree to know that something utterly great was going on.

And she didn't do anything fancy, either, but it looked so flowing, so effortless on the part of horse and rider alike.

Do I sound like I'm ranting? Well, I probably am.

Frau Schwetman herself took on a bearing that was regal. She seemed, in fact, to grow in height and slenderize. On the ground, remember, she was just a little dumpling. On the ground she was shaped a little bit like me.

I watched her communicate with the animal, watched the horse's ears twitching ever so slightly as Frau Schwetman made little bitty adjustments with her legs and seat, little compliments, little corrections with her hands. It was as if the horse was listening intently to every breath that the woman took.

Not that any of this manipulation would have been obvious to anyone who wasn't looking for it, mind. To the average onlooker, Katerina Schwetman would have seemed perfectly still.

Did I say she wasn't doing anything fancy? Well, that was a kind of warm-up. Shortly afterward she was doing passage—a slow motion kind of trot—and piaffe— which, you'll remember, is an animated trot in place.

And that wasn't the end of her display. Eventually she was doing tempi changes every other stride.

I guess I ought to explain.

When a horse canters—that's like a gallop only slower and more controlled—he leads with one front leg. One front leg, that is, reaches out farther than the other.

In a flying change of lead, which is very hard to do on command, he'll be leading with his left leg, say, and then, at a signal from the rider, change to leading with his right. Well, what Frau Schwetman was able to do was to get him to do this repeatedly every other stride, like left left, right right, left left, right right. It looks as if the horse is skipping.

Then, as if that hadn't been enough, she did *one* tempis, left, right, left right, left right.

We all applauded and Edie applauded loudest of all.

When the ride was over, Frau Schwetman—in her granny years, after all—wasn't even breathing hard. The gelding, however, was lathered. I took the reins and prepared to lead the horse away.

I would have to walk the horse for half an hour, at least, to cool him down before he could be hosed. He seemed happy, though, depleted in a wonderful, Hey-I'm-an-Athlete kind of way.

Meanwhile, I heard Edie repeating again and again that her horse had never looked so good.

"Ah, *ja*," came the guttural response. I turned back to see Frau Schwetman wag a finger at her hostess. "So he should look always." Then she wagged at everyone in general. "So should all your horses look, *ja*?"

So it went as the day wore on. The riders came at forty-five-minute intervals, and Frau Schwetman coached them without much pause. I would always be nearly out of earshot, either hosing or walking the preceding horse. Occasionally I caught a word or two, as when Frau Schwetman advised a rider to "use the other sit-bone." Once or twice I heard her say, "Very better," when a rider had improved.

The horses were pretty spectacular to start with, and the riders weren't bad. They were all far more advanced than I could even hope to be. Still, after about a half hour, Frau Schwetman would get up on the horses herself and then the horses, one and all, went from pretty spectacular to *very* spectacular.

It sounds Disneylandish, I know, but it was as if she inspired these animals just by sitting on top of them. And I'm not exaggerating either. The minute she'd settle into the saddle and take up the reins—even before she'd placed her feet into the stirrups—the horses would kind of come to attention. As if she'd delivered a silent *achtung!* with her seat. So many times you see horses going through their paces in a desultory way. With Frau Schwetman on board, their whole attitude changed; they seemed to *want* to go forward, to *want* to perform for her.

I even found myself thinking that she was *worth* two hundred dollars an hour.

And I found myself wondering how old Plum would

look with her up there in the saddle. It would be worth two hundred dollars to find out.

Except that it was out of the question, of course. I didn't have two hundred dollars in my account. And over and above this, it would be a breach of manners to ask the clinician to do something she hadn't contracted to do. Particularly since I was a lowly groom.

All of this was before Frau Schwetman wounded me in the patriotism. Which came at the lunch break, when I was officially introduced.

"And this," Edie enthused, "is Robin Vaughan."

Katerina Schwetman extended a plump hand. "Von . . . ?" She waited for the rest of my name.

"Oh, no, that *is* my name," I said, laughing. "My whole name, unless you count my maiden name, which is Rendell, but of course being my maiden name, it wouldn't be *after* Vaughan anyway, it would come in before it, as in—" Babble, babble, babble.

And Frau Schwetman mercifully interrupted, though with a dismissive wave of her pudgy hand. "Ah, *ja*, Ame-rica."

Well, all right, it wasn't burning the flag or anything, but it rubbed me wrong, okay?

One of the other riders came up behind Edie and the Frau. "Coffee's perked," she sang.

This garnered a smile from Frau Schwetman.

"Just help yourself," Edie said.

The smile froze, then disintegrated. It was replaced by a look of hauteur.

Poor Edie continued, totally unaware, "We've got sugar, we've got Nutrasweet, we've got real cream."

One of the other women saw what I had seen. She toadied right over and said, "Let me *get* you a cup, Frau Schwetman. Would you like sugar? Cream?"

Nanoseconds, that was all it took, and Frau Schwetman's smile was back in place and everything was hunky-dory. Except that after *this* episode especially, I just couldn't see Nika Ballinger getting this woman to let her wear her FEI clothes. I mean, democratic the woman was not.

CHAPTER 12

Thus far everyone except our aristocratic clinician seemed more or less down to earth. Rich, for sure, but regular people all the same. Except maybe for Elsbeth, the woman who rode immediately following lunch. The one who wouldn't have me—or anyone else who hadn't had a blood test, I guess—handle her horse.

Elsbeth was a bad rider on an animal who deserved far more. Her hands jiggled and her body swayed and pounded against the horse's back and her legs swung this way and that. Through it all, the horse did relatively okay work. But that didn't stop Elsbeth from bashing him across the shoulder with her long dressage whip at three-stride intervals or gouging him with her spurs.

Frau Schwetman watched as Elsbeth warmed up, a frown deepening with every step that the horse-and-rider combination took. Finally she called, "Enough."

Elsbeth continued as if Frau Schwetman hadn't said a thing.

"Halt, please."

Frau Schwetman walked up to Elsbeth and took hold of the whip. Elsbeth didn't seem to want to relinquish it. She and the frau tugged at it, and meanwhile the long-suffering horse continued to stand beneath his rider.

Frau Schwetman succeeded in getting the crop away. With a smile, she hurled it off to the side. Then she unbuckled and slipped off the woman's spur. Left. Then the right. She flung those as well. "You will continue, please," she instructed.

Elsbeth slammed her boots into the horse's side, and despite this, the animal moved cheerily away.

Frau Schwetman walked back to the clutch of chairs.

Everyone stared as Frau Schwetman sat, saying nothing.

Perplexed, Elsbeth continued to ride around.

Frau Schwetman said nothing.

After ten excruciatingly uncomfortable minutes, Elsbeth rode over to where Frau Schwetman sat. "I don't know what you want me to do," she whined. When she got no reply, she turned her attention to the audience. "What does she want me to do?"

No one said a word.

"Well, I'm leaving," Elsbeth huffed, yanking on her horse's mouth and dismounting.

No one moved.

"I'm sorry I ever came here," Elsbeth spat as she led her horse away.

It reminded me of this movie about West Point where the cadets imposed The Silence. And somehow we all participated in it, watching until Elsbeth was out of sight.

It was Edie who spoke first. "Well," she said, looking at her watch. "We won't have the next horse until three-forty-five, so if anyone would like to freshen up . . ."

Frau Katerina Schwetman hadn't budged, hadn't even blinked.

So okay, I thought, I'd forgive her that America remark.

* * *

From the spectators' standpoint Frau Schwetman's next encounter was even livelier. The rider, Jeanette, was a cheerleader type. Which is to say that she kept up a running dialogue with her horse as she rode, and I don't mean sotto voce. "All right, all *right*," she called out as her horse lengthened down the long side. "That's good, that's so so good," as the animal collected again. "Not fast, no so fast," around the turn. "Slower, yes, slower here, yes, ah, yes."

Katerina Schwetman turned to the audience. "One cannot but wonder," she said, her blue eyes twinkling like Santa's, "what this one is like in the more intimate moments, *ja*?"

That did it. I was a confirmed lifetime member of the Katerina Schwetman fan club. No kidding, I wanted to have T-shirts made.

I took advantage of the break to place a call extolling the Schwetman virtues to Lola. It was automatic for me to call her. It didn't even occur to me when I did that she was mad at me, or that I'd had these little glints of suspicion about her as I'd gone along. The thing is, I wanted to share what I was seeing with someone who mattered and who was horsey, too.

I got her answering machine, but I talked at length anyway. I told her how totally amazing Frau Schwetman was, and how she made the horses all look so fabulous and how she got them all to do fantastic things. And glancing quickly around to make sure no one could overhear, I added, "And you should see the way she deals with dingbats, too. Whooee, impressive. Anyway, how Nika got into Frau Schwetman's clothes and up on her horse is beyond me, if she did."

At which point the door flew open and at least five

of the women riders came in, so I quit. And anyway, it was just as well, because I didn't think I'd told Lola what Manuel had said about the camera and so none of this would have made a lot of sense. Or *had* I told her? Oh, well. I threw in a fast, "Gotta run, the life of a Braedock groom leaves very little time for idle telephone chitchat," and hung up.

I ran up to the barn to check on Plum. On the way I was happy to see that in addition to Mother and my own trailer, there was one other ratty old rig amid the splendiferous assortment of matching truck-and-trailer ensembles parked beside the place. Who, I wondered, owned the other eyesore?

One of the other women came up behind me. "Amazing, isn't it?" she said.

"The clinic? Frau Schwetman? What?"

"Well, all of those, yes but I meant Edie's rig." The woman gestured at the very truck and trailer I'd been eyeing. "It belongs to the Conovers," she told me.

"I can sympathize," I said. "The green Dodge and that blue thing, that's mine."

"Insert foot in mouth," the woman apologized.

"Not really," I soothed.

"Which one is Katerina Schwetman's?" I asked.

"The maroon job over there. Or at least it's the one she's using while she's here in Texas."

On closer inspection, the truck and trailer that Frau Schwetman was using proved to be from Windsor Rentals—at least that's what the stenciled letters on the side of both elements read. I made a mental note to call Windsor and find out when she'd signed up to borrow the thing. I wasn't exactly sure why I needed to know, but I figured it might help nail whether or not she'd been at Nika's on the day of Nika's death.

I didn't want to be seen trying doors and trailer compartments, so I contented myself with a brief look inside as I stood next to the cab of the truck.

Bingo!

I could see a video camera still affixed to a tripod lying on its side just behind the seats.

So maybe Manuel was right.

At the barn I ascertained that Plum was happy and had water and hay. I also noted that the Braedock stable staff hadn't left a speck of manure to be seen. If you don't know horses, you probably don't realize that they poop continuously, mountains of it. Picking up after a horse that well would probably mean policing the stalls at ten-minute intervals. I was duly impressed.

I hied it to the arena, where a dutiful husband was setting up to record his wife's clinic ride. Hovering beside him was Katerina Schwetman, obviously asking questions about the camera and its use. The man pointed at this lever and that and Frau Schwetman nodded her understanding.

"Here, watch." The man aimed at his wife, approaching now with her freshly tacked up horse. He zoomed in on the woman's backside as she mounted. You could hear the zoom mechanism at work. "She won't like this one bit," he said delightedly. "Now," he said to Katerina, "let me show you."

He indicated the viewfinder. Katerina Schwetman seemed hesitant. "Come on," he said, "I'll play back what I just shot."

"Play back?"

"Right. You can watch it through here just like it's on the television back at the house. You can watch it through here, except that it'll be little and there won't be color."

Frau Schwetman watched the fragment of tape and

then waxed appreciative. But if the camera in her truck was her own, why wouldn't she have already known about these standard features?

The day's riding was over by five. The group made plans to drive en masse to a local pizzeria, but I demurred. I hadn't ridden Plum yet. Plus it had been twenty-four hours or more since I'd had any sleep.

I went to the third-floor room that had been assigned to me and fell back on the bed without even removing the spread.

My plan was to nap for an hour or so. Then ride, then snoop. I wanted a closer look at the camera in Frau Schwetman's truck just to see if it in any way indicated that it had belonged to Nika. I don't know what I expected to find. Maybe a social security number engraved on it the way those Crime Watch programs say to do. Even the presence of a social security number would have to mean that it didn't belong to the Frau.

The next thing I knew I was watching Elsbeth being forced off a ship. The waters surrounding the ship were filled with shark fins zigging and zagging, but Elsbeth was inching toward the railing nonetheless.

Then Frau Katerina Schwetman came into view. She had a video camera in one hand and a riding whip in the other. She was driving Elsbeth toward the rail with the whip and filming the woman's progress with the camera.

"No, no," Elsbeth shouted. Then there was a splash.

I awakened suddenly, perplexed by the darkness of the room. I had evidently slept longer than I'd meant to. I tried to see my watch, but couldn't, and despite my groping, I couldn't locate a lamp.

Splash! The sound was as loud as it had been in my dream. It had come from outside, but way down below.

I edged my way toward the window and found myself staring down at a lighted rectangle that was the pool. A lone swimmer was silhouetted against the aqua backdrop, but from the water's glow I could see that several people had gathered near the pool.

Everyone was back from dinner, it seemed. I reasoned that it must be at least nine o'clock. And I still hadn't managed to work my mare.

I had to pass the parking area on my way to the barn. I decided to grab the camera from Frau Schwetman's and have my look-see. I had forgotten that in most vehicles, vehicles younger and in better shape than Mother, the overhead light comes on when you open the door.

It was like being on stage. And spotlighted there, I had no way of knowing who might lurk in the surrounding darkness. For all I knew, every single person at the pool could have spotted that light going on and Frau Katerina Schwetman might well have been one of them.

But I took the camera and tripod out anyway, trying to separate the two parts. I yanked and pushed and twisted things, all the while telling myself how stupid I was to be doing this. I must have hit eject, because a videotape cassette popped out.

I would have to settle for that. I put the camera and tripod back where it had been, slid the cassette under the sweatshirt I was carrying, and moved off.

The barn was dark. I felt along the first panel I encountered and the lights came on.

Plum greeted me before I'd even reached her stall, her soft nicker chiding, "Where've you been?" I put my sweatshirt and the video down on the floor beside her stall and got my grooming tools out. I brushed Plum quickly, then tacked up and led her into the aisle.

I wasn't as lucky finding the lights to the indoor arena. The only switch that I could locate illuminated some recessed lighting near the floor. It cast an eerie yellowish glow.

Still, it was better than nothing. It was, in fact, workable once my eyes adjusted to it. I got on and walked Plum around the arena's dimly lit perimeter.

She felt creaky, probably because of having spent the day in first the trailer, then the stall. Not lame, mind you, but creaky, reluctant to really reach out and move. At home she's outside all day, and so she never really gets quite as stiff as she seemed to be now.

I asked her to walk big for a while and then, when she loosened, began to trot. My reins were long loops along her neck. I let her poke her head out and move like a hunter, first traveling in the direction that is her good side, the left, then to the right.

Finally, after fifteen minutes or so, I began to reel her in to invite her onto the bit.

Usually she'll do this quite readily, almost as soon as I pick up the reins. Tonight, however, I was eager to put into practice what I'd seen Katerina Schwetman do.

Not that I was going to attempt tempi changes and piaffe and whatnot. I was, and probably would always be, a far, far cry from that. No, I was going to bend Plum around my leg and let her put herself on the bit.

On the bit.

These are the three most important words in the dressage rider's lexicon. What they mean is not easy to explain.

Most folks think of it as meaning tracking up behind— that is, the back legs reaching well under the horse—while traveling with an arched neck in front. It *looks* like that, to be sure.

Trouble is, the two have to be, literally, connected. In fact, that is what was so impressive about Katerina Schwetman's various rides. The connection was there, painless and continuous and apparent.

I know, I know—you don't know from horses and this is all gibberish to you, but try this: Think about a suspension bridge, about the way all the guy wires work to keep the bridge up, think about the constant tension they maintain to do that.

Having a horse really on the bit is like that. The reins are the guy wires and the rider's arms are the cables and the horse's body is the actual bridge and the whole thing is there because the connection is solid and perfect and unbroken.

In real-life dressage, this is the ideal, maybe attained for three or four footfalls at a time before the rider does something clumsy and messes it up.

Or else it's faked. The horse looks as though he's on the bit, but the flow of energy isn't really there, animating every cell in the horse's body every single moment of the time. The horse isn't, as they say, *coming through*.

There is, of course, a German word for this: *Durchlassigkeit*.

Okay, so maybe you're still not impressed, but here's another thing to consider: The rider, to maintain this very delicate balance with the horse, has to have absolute control of his own body. Every movement that the rider makes—I mean a squeeze with a calf muscle, a weighting of this or that seatbone, a quirking of a single finger—has to be on purpose, has to be made in order to complement the way the horse is moving.

And the horse, don't forget, is moving all the time.

This—the intensity and the challenge of it—is why dressage sucks so many of us in.

And even those who start out, shall we say *impurely*, maybe only doing it because the horse looks so *pretty*, eventually learn that dressage is a mystical as well as a physical thing, like the Sphinx or like the *Mona Lisa*'s smile.

All of which sounds terribly lofty when I'm up here trying to do a decent leg yield, which is about as basic as you can get.

I tried it again, remembering some of the body English I'd heard Frau Schwetman advise when working with the others, my torso as straight ahead as I could get it, but my right shoulder back, my right calf tapping.

And while it was a better yield than I'd been getting, it wasn't quite complete, so I tried once more, tapping harder.

Worse.

And to make matters even more excruciating, that now-familiar Germanic voice rang out in what I'd thought was the deserted riding hall, "Shtop!"

I shtopped.

And Frau Schwetman came out of the shadows and up beside my horse. She reached up and poked me in the stomach. "Let go," she said. "Shtop with the pinching and the pushing and let go."

Then she stood in an absurd position, hips thrust forward. "Like so," she said, "like so."

I made my own hips in the saddle do the same. And Plum responded, her back coming up beneath my seat.

"Jawohl," Frau Schwetman told me. "Now go." She stepped backward, and Plum walked on with a vigor I hadn't known she had. "Now the same as before only

less with the leg, *ja*? And more back with the shoulder.''

Plum swept rather than inched, as had always been her custom, into the movement. "Holy Guacamole," I said.

"Now try the other direction," Frau Schwetman told me.

I did, with Plum offering the same deliciously sweet response.

Katerina Schwetman assumed that ludicrous hips-first position yet again. She patted her mons veneris. "Is all here," she said. "If you will be loose, the horse will be free."

I wondered why she hadn't bothered telling any of the others this major secret. On the other hand, I didn't feel like announcing it to the world. I just wanted to marvel at the energy I was able to get Plum to produce.

Frau Schwetman came up beside me when I halted, patting Plum. "She is an old girl, is she not?"

"Yes."

"She is what? Thoroughbred?"

"Yes," I told her, "off the track."

"You do well with her," she said, "considering."

I knew what she meant. Considering that the mare is old and cranky and semiarthritic and not bred to do this the way the other horses in the clinic had been bred.

"A pity you do not own the gray," she said, referring to Elsbeth's stunning though put-upon horse.

"Oh, well," I replied.

"May I?" Frau Schwetman seemed to be indicating that she'd like to get on Plum.

"Oh, yes!" I jumped off so fast that I think Plum thought that her saddle had caught fire.

Watching Katerina Schwetman mount at such close range made me aware of how stiff the woman herself had grown with the years. She winced as she propelled herself up and into the saddle.

"Does it hurt you to ride?" I asked.

"I do not think of that," she said as she started Plum on a twenty-meter circle at trot.

I could see her settling into the horse's movement with visible effort. Still, she demanded that the horse move fully and freely beneath her.

Soon those hind legs of Plum's were chugging right along and Plum was hunkered down onto the bit like a champ. Frau Schwetman brought her down the long side in shoulder-in. I was astonished. What the woman was getting from Plum was leagues away from the mincy-mincy steps that I always got, the mincy-mincy steps you see almost everybody getting, even in the show ring.

Instead, Plum just boomed along as though she couldn't tell the difference between a regular trot and this lateral one that, just as the name implies, asks the horse to keep one shoulder in so that the front legs cross, while the hind legs keep on going as if the front-end business weren't happening. It's a suppling thing for horses, shoulder-in, like yoga is for us. It loosens the horse up.

By this time, too, Frau Schwetman's musculature had loosened as well and she was back to the same smooth and elegant rider that I'd earlier observed.

"Plum looks great!" I shouted, and Frau Schwetman responded with a brief hint of a smile.

When she brought Plum to a halt and dismounted, she made quite a fuss over her, rifling her mane and stroking her neck and calling her a grand old girl. But then she said to me, "You will buy the gray horse, perhaps."

"No." I laughed, thinking of how much that horse would have to cost. "I have no money." I indicated Plum. "This is the only horse I can afford."

"Is a pity," she told me, running Plum's stirrups up and loosening the girth.

Of course I've yearned after a thousand other horses. It would be hard not to when they're everywhere around me practically night and day. Horses who are taller, horses who go forward with practically no effort from the rider at all. Horses with natural overstride, horses with great big floating trots. Horses like the ones housed here, or those that Nika owned.

"You taught Nika Ballinger, didn't you?" I said. It probably sounded very out of the blue considering the subject we had been discussing.

Frau Schwetman tensed. "I know no one by this name," she said.

"I mean Veronika Ballinger," I explained. "In Austin."

"You are mistaken," she said. Her entire manner had changed. Her words had a clipped and very formal sound to them now. And there was no trace of the camaraderie we'd begun to share only moments ago.

"Look," I said, "I'm sorry if I—" I wasn't quite sure what I was going to say, but I wanted her to know that I hadn't meant anything untoward by my question.

But she interrupted me, saying, "I must go," and turning on her heel before I could even get a simple thank-you out of my mouth.

"Thank you," I called at her back. "I really appreciate the help you . . ." but she was out of sight.

No one seemed to be about when I got back down to the house. I used the time to track down the number of Jeet's Padre Island hotel. He'd probably tried to call me a dozen times, I reasoned. So I'd better tell him where I was. I would give an annotated version, of course, a version that wouldn't refer to Nika Ballinger's murder or anything horsey.

I got the hotel all right, but the operator insisted on giving me the direct-dial number to his room. "Can't you just—" I began before the woman pulled the plug on me.

It's okay, I told myself. Long distance to people like the Conovers was nothing.

Sure enough, the first question out of Jeet's mouth was, "Where are you?"

"Houston," I said. "It's a long story."

"Yeah, I'll bet. Hey, listen, about your little joke . . ." He let his voice trail off.

"What joke?"

"Come on, Robin. You know what I'm talking about."

"I do not."

"The garment bag. Dean liked it especially. He asked me if I planned to model the stuff."

"What stuff?"

"The little-girl clothes? The pinafore and the *Alice in Wonderland* dress?"

"Jeet, I swear, I . . ." and then it hit me. He was talking about the bag I'd stolen from Nika's closet. How had he gotten hold of it, though?

I remembered myself draping it over the back of one of the chairs. I remembered, too, seeing his garment bag there, too. He'd probably put his down on top of Nika's and he'd taken them both.

But little-girl clothes?

"Are they real little, like doll's clothes," I asked him, "or what?"

"They're grown-up size, hon, but they're . . . oh,

hey, I've got to run, my ride is here. My limo, I should say. Can you believe that? They send a limo for us and they . . . talk to you soon, have fun in Houston, and I love you.''

''I love you, too.'' But once more I was talking to a dead connection. I sighed and replaced the receiver in the cradle and turned to find Frau Katerina Schwetman framed in the doorway.

''Those clothes,'' I said, not really to her, but to myself.

''You are impertinent,'' she said, her pupils beading up and all but turning red.

I have trouble hitting it off with some people, but actually, with her, I thought I had been doing okay. Until I'd mentioned Nika, of course.

''These clothes you spoke of.'' She came closer now, observing my response very carefully. ''What was it about them you wished to say?''

''Nothing, I, uh . . .'' I laughed uncomfortably. ''I just, uh, found out about a friend of mine who wears, I don't know, uh, little girl's clothes.''

''People are so very odd,'' Katerina Schwetman said. ''It's curious. They think the clothes make the thing happen. It is this way with riding clothes, as if to buy the top hat, the shadbelly, will make the movements come easily at last.''

So she was testing me to see if I knew about Nika wearing the FEI clothes. What else could it have been? That's what I got for mentioning Nika's name.

Frau Schwetman had obviously decided to check me out, follow me down here, and be cagey and subtle. Well, I'd have to play the game. Be cagey and subtle right back. Except as you have probably guessed, this is not my strong suit.

"Would *you* ever let anyone wear, uh, your riding clothes?" I asked.

Her chin jerked upward. "Why should I do that?" she asked. She actually began to step around me as if I were on display, eyeing me the whole while.

"I don't know."

"Perhaps for a photograph?" she supplied.

"Oh, right!" I said, but not sarcastically. As if I were saying, "Oh, of course!" By now I was thinking that either she knows I know about the picture of Nika or else we are having the dumbest conversation ever on record.

"A photograph on my Spier," she continued.

"Your . . . spear?" I wasn't sure I'd caught that one. She hadn't used a simple *S* sound, she'd used a *Sh*. But that still didn't make much sense.

"Spier. My stallion. He is here right now, in a stall next to your Plum." She pronounced my horse's name as "Plume."

Hmmm. "So let me get this straight," I tried. "You let people wear your clothes and get their picture taken sitting on your stallion." Well, it beats giving pony rides, I guess.

Bam! She slammed her hand against her thigh so hard that I'm sure that underneath her breeches, it left a bright red mark. "There are times," she said, in a way that was way too controlled, "when one might ask this. One might ask it thinking that one has—how do you say it?—levers."

She meant leverage. And boy, if there was ever a person out there gathering up info to be used as leverage, it was Nika. I thought of those envelopes I'd found in her ivory box, of the words she'd collected for the one she had designated mine, of the tape she had in Lola's. And then I thought of the envelope with the *K* on it, the one that held the magazine cover featuring Melissa Song.

Melissa Song—at least Frau Schwetman's attitude toward her—must have been the leverage that got Nika Ballinger into Frau Schwetman's FEI duds and on board Spier. Jeez, maybe Frau Schwetman was even the one who had burned through the picture, burned through Melissa's face and crotch. And Nika, being Nika, knew heavy-duty blackmail material when she saw it!

But that was stupid. Frau Schwetman didn't even smoke. And mutilating a magazine cover didn't seem like the sort of thing Frau Schwetman would do even if Melissa Song could outride the Schwetman twins. I mean, didn't she love dressage? Didn't she love the sport? Wouldn't she be happy just to see someone riding that well?

Even while I was thinking this, I heard my voice asking her, "Do you smoke?" and in a very pointed way, too.

I watched her eyes turn into lasers bent on boring into my own. "On occasion," she said, "a small cigar."

If a steno had been in the room, taking down the words, it would have sounded very innocent, except that it wasn't. It wasn't at all. Frau Schwetman's eyes and the tone of her voice said clearly and unmistakably that I'd gone way too far.

Frau Schwetman regarded me the way she might a cockroach. "Now you are thinking to use the levers, too." She shook her head, then cast her eyes around the kitchen. I saw where they'd come to rest. On a wooden knife rack.

My heart began to pound. But this was crazy, wasn't it? I mean, how would she explain hacking me to death in the kitchen?

The phone rang. I dived for it and gave a kind of anguished hello. It was Lo. "Oh, so you heard," she said.

Frau Schwetman had taken the smallest of the knives and was innocently paring one of her fingernails.

"Heard what?" I asked.

"About Ron. They've arrested him. Something about how long it took him to dial nine-one-one. Hey, are you all right?"

Frau Schwetman smiled at me.

"I guess I am," I said.

"Conover's representing him. It was on the news."

"Conover," I said.

"You know your hostess, Edie? Greenback. Her husband."

"Small world," I said.

"Robin, are you sure you're all right? You sound the way you sounded that day you stayed out in the sun too long."

Frau Schwetman had replaced the knife. She hadn't even rinsed it, I noted.

"No," I assured her, "I'm okay. I can even do a really good leg yield now."

"But are you actually *in* the clinic?"

"No, but . . ."

"Oh, I get it. You're learning through osmosis."

"Well, not exactly, I . . ." But maybe I'd imagined my private session with Frau Schwetman the way I had her being just about ready to have at me with a cleaver right there in the Conover kitchen.

I hit the sack and realized how long it had been since I'd been under sheets. I was just dozing off when I realized that I hadn't retrieved the video from the barn. It was still up there outside Plum's stall underneath my sweatshirt. *Do it*, I commanded myself, but another part of me was at war. *In the morning*, the other part, the stronger part, said. It wasn't likely that Frau Schwetman would miss it, and it wasn't as though it contained anything crucial. Knowing Nika as I did, it was probably just another one of her abysmal rides, this time being coached by superstar Schwetman herself.

I dreamed of Nika, Nika in her pinafore and saddle shoes. "I want my daddy," she was saying. Fortunately, only Ron's voice appeared.

"Have you been a bad girl?" he asked.

"I'm a good girl, Daddy," Nika said. "I'm a very good girl."

I woke up feeling that I had been forced to watch X-rated movies. Still, what I'd dreamed seemed another answer to why Nika owned those clothes. The kiddie clothes, I mean. Forget her wanting a baby. Forget her creating the room she'd never had as a kid. It tied in with all those surgeries she'd had, too, didn't it? The frantic search for youth.

And if that's what Nika had to do—dress up in clothes like that to please Ron—it was no wonder that she'd been a bitch on wheels with the rest of the world.

Nika and now Suzie. Would Suzie have to dress like that, too? Would I have been willing to do it if it meant living in a place like Cliffside and owning all of those fancy animals?

I didn't know what time it was, but the house was dark except for the kitchen light, which I'd left on. I called Lola anyway.

"You know," she said, "I just got over being mad at you. This call doesn't help."

"Lo, I had to talk to you," I said. Every wisp of suspicion that I'd ever had regarding her—about the tractor, about Ron, about the way she'd brushed me off when I said I was coming over—was gone. I had made up my mind once and for all that Lola was my friend, my best friend, and that was that.

So I told her about the clothes Jeet had taken with him and what my dream suggested that it meant. "What do *you* think?" I asked.

"I definitely think there's something wrong with Ron," Lo said. "And I think it's sexual, too. I think it's pretty likely that he and Nika had a kind of Daddy's-little-girl thing."

"Oh, yuck," I said, remembering that telephone conversation when Ron had gone on and on about how Nika had been his little girl. "But that's so personal? How could you possibly know?" What can I say? I guess suspicion ought to be my middle name. I'm a born interrogator, that's all.

"Robin, really, don't ask."

"You mean . . . ?" The entrance at Ron's office suddenly appeared to me. The tiles had called the place the Albright Building. But if Lo had slept with him, she'd still own the place, wouldn't she? Wouldn't that have been the trade? "You mean you slept with him?"

"No," Lo said, but with a hesitation in her voice. "But I almost would have at one point—a very low point—except he flat out wasn't interested."

"Wasn't interested?"

"I don't mean I asked him, but I didn't get any of those vibes, you know what I mean? I mean, I just knew I wouldn't get anywhere that way."

"Was this before or after, you know, Nika and . . ." I couldn't bring myself to say Cody, knowing now what I knew about how Lola felt about him.

"After." There was ice in her voice. I thought she'd slam the phone down on me again.

"Wait, Lola," I said, "Ron cheated you, didn't he? He cheated you out of your tractor and your building."

"Cheated me? Are you kidding? If he hadn't bought that building, I'd have lost it. I owed so much in taxes on it that it wasn't funny, plus the place was a wreck. Listen, Robin, you've got it all wrong. Ron *saved* me, saved this farm by buying that building."

"And what about the tractor?"

"God, I just ran an ad in the paper. I don't even remember who bought it, but the money sure came in handy at the time."

After that ego-depleting conversation—I mean, was I ever, *consciously* I mean, right about anything ever?

Which reminded me of the video. I knew I ought to go up and get it, but the fact is, I wasn't sure where Frau Schwetman was right then. For all I knew, she could be lurking down one of the stable aisles. And with my phenomenal luck, she'd appear again when I had the tape in my hand.

I stood there feeling utterly miserable, wishing someone would hug me and tell me everything would be all right.

Someone. Jeet.

I dialed, but after the first ring I remembered that it was late and that Lo hadn't been exactly pleased that the phone had rung and that possibly Jeet wouldn't be either, and hung up.

Everything will be all right, I told myself, and headed back upstairs to bed.

At sunrise I was all set to go up to the barn to reclaim the videotape when I heard the voices of several people all at once. What had they done? Risen at four?

"Ah, here you are," Edie called to me quite cheerily. "Good news," she said. "Elsbeth isn't coming

back and you can have her slot today at least. Tomorrow
I'll have to start calling up the waiting list, but today
just give me a check and the ride is yours."

"For two hundred dollars," I confirmed.

Edie grinned. "That's right."

She followed me as I searched for my purse and then
watched me as I plumbed its depths looking for my
checkbook and a pen, too. So much for my theory about
her knowing I was churchmouse poor.

I started to write.

"Just make it out to Braedock," Edie said.

"Oh, rats," I told her. "I've already written 'Katerina Schwetman.' And it's my last check, too." No lie.

"Oh, well. That's okay. Just give it to me anyway."

I continued writing, sneaking a peek at the clock.
Somewhere, at a breakfast table in South Padre, Jeet
Vaughan was clutching his rear end, the back trouser
pocket where he kept his wallet. He was, I'm sure,
wondering why he had this terrible stabbing pain there.
I'd have to check with him about the time.

When we reached the arena, however, Katerina
Schwetman announced that during the period that would
have been taken up by Elsbeth's ride, she was going to
give a very special presentation. So, no lesson for me.

She would bring out her stallion, Spier, and on long
reins he'd perform various airs above the ground.

The audience gasped. Airs above the ground are the
ne plus ultra of dressage. They aren't called for in any
of the tests, not even the Grand Prix and Grand Prix
Special, which are ridden in the Olympics. You may
have seen the Lippizaners, the horses owned by the
Spanish Riding School of Vienna, doing them, but that's
probably the only time you have. They are out of the
reach of most horses, most trainers, too.

Frau Schwetman looked at me. "The groom," she said, "will perhaps bring Spier to me at the proper hour."

"Oh, gladly," I said, my smile as wide as Gloria Vanderbilt's. I was quite a bit more chipper thinking that I was going to get my two-hundred-dollar check back and therefore be legal again.

"With surcingle and long reins," she said.

"And where would those be?" I asked.

She didn't answer right away. She took time, first, to let her blue eyes bore deep into my soul. "In my truck," she said. "You know of course which one it is. I do not lock it."

I felt that all-too-familiar wave of heat wash from my neck straight up to my hairline. I nodded yes.

She noted this, then turned to the audience. "I had, in my truck, a cassette of these movements done by Spier. It is no longer there."

Everybody stopped talking and looked at everyone else. Katerina Schwetman waited until all eyes were back on her. "Someone here, perhaps"—and this is where she turned to me and gestured with a nod of her head—"will find it and replace it."

Now everyone looked at me.

Having achieved this, she clapped her hands together. "I will have my first horse now," she called, as though none of this business about the purloined videotape had meant anything.

I know I should have returned the video at once, but I was afraid now that someone would see me doing it and know that I had been the thief. So I left it lying where it was, beneath my sweatshirt on my tack trunk just outside Plum's stall.

As I approached Spier, who seemed about twice

Plum's size, for his gala performance that afternoon, I didn't even so much as glance at the spot where the video lay.

I hadn't any experience with stallions and was a wee bit wary. Spier proved, however, to be a total lamb. He, like Plum, had certain body spots he wanted to make sure I covered, and he twisted himself beneath my ministrations to make sure I got to them. When I rubbed his brisket—which is the flat area between his front legs—he groaned and rolled his eyes back in his head.

"Good boy," I said, using the brush extra hard.

Edie came up out of nowhere. "I was planning to return your check," she said, "but Frau Schwetman tells me that you had a private session with her here last night."

Great.

"Well, that's true," I said, "but I hadn't really asked for it. She just kind of materialized while I was working on my own and started coaching me." Please, please, I was inwardly pleading. "I can't say it wasn't worth the money, though."

Edie beamed. "I'm glad you agree. I wouldn't have charged you for it since it wasn't your idea and all, but the others in the clinic felt it would only be fair."

"Well, then," I said. Jeet was probably getting that pain in the old hip pocket again.

"Let me help you with those reins." Edie slipped inside the stall and gave me a much-needed hand. I wondered if she knew I had stolen the video. The thief would be someone like me. Someone who had tried to get away with a Schwetman freebie.

We walked Spier toward the arena, Edie on one side, I on the other. We had to really step to keep up with him. He seemed far more eager than any horse I'd ever walked beside.

He proved to be a total ham, too. The minute he saw the audience, he began to prance and toss his head. Edie and I tugged on the long reins, but we were totally ineffective. Fortunately, Katerina Schwetman took over and we sat to watch.

She stood behind him, longe whip in hand. She would tap, and Spier would move left or right or forward as she wished. She would call out to him as she worked, usually a series of *ja*s with a "good boy" thrown in.

He snorted as he worked. And he was showing off, too. You could tell. And God, but he was something! When she asked him to canter out of the halt, the result was immediate. And the canter was so collected that Frau Schwetman was able, easily, to *walk* behind. The halt itself? It required but a soft, muttered sound.

Then she merely flicked her wrist and we could see Spier gathering himself more and more still. Gathering himself until his massive head and chest lifted off the ground, his forelegs in the sky, his rear legs crouched— a perfect, classical levade.

There was a group *Aaaah!* as we realized the quality of the performance we were watching.

Frau Schwetman guided Spier through another levade and then an immediate courbette, a series of hops taken in levade, a movement that even the Spanish Riding School considered the most difficult.

And now she talked to Spier, who was back with all fours on the ground. "You will be a good boy, won't you, Spier?" she said, patting him, observing the patches of sweat on his stifle and the thick lather that had formed between his rear legs, both sure signs that his hindquarters were really pumping. *"Ja, ja."*

Then she crooked a finger at me. "You will please to come here," she said.

"Me?"

"Ja."

I eased off my chair and walked across the sandy surface to the spot where Spier stood, obviously steadying himself for something big.

Frau Schwetman looked at me with her ice-blue soul-boring eyes yet again. "You will take the reins," she said, and I did.

I could feel the audience's envy. Their curiosity, too.

"You will stand here," she said, directing me by the shoulders to a spot behind the horse. Then she backed away. "He is ready," she said. "Just hold the reins so and I will give the command."

I looked away from her to Spier. He seemed nervous, his hindquarters shifting slightly left to right to left. I looked back to Katerina Schwetman and she held my gaze as though attempting to communicate with me on the subliminal plane.

It scared me.

I don't know why.

I began to sweat profusely, big salty drops rolling down across my forehead and into my eyes.

I could feel the sweat dripping down into my bra and staining my shirt across my back and under my arms.

I had to one-hand the reins in order to swipe at my forehead and my eyes.

Frau Schwetman looked triumphant. "Here," she said, grabbing my shoulders again and moving me off a little to the side. "Is better."

The command she gave was unlike the others, a loud bark that was quite distinct. It was still reverberating when Spier landed square on the ground again and stood, heaving slightly, waiting for his praise.

The applause for this—a capriole, a huge move upward into the air, a huge thrust with the hind legs while airborne—was thunderous. He seemed to absorb it, take it as his due. Off toward his rump, Katerina Schwetman was, again, looking hard at me. I felt myself blinking as if to ward off her gaze. Inside I was quaking.

"You may take him away," she said, unsnapping the long reins and attaching an ordinary lead. She began issuing a list of orders. "Wash him, the legs especially. Let him graze in hand until he is dry. Then liniment on the flexor tendons, *ja*, stroking only down. You will show me that you know where this is, and how it should be done."

I knelt at Spier's feet and ran the heels of my hands along the appropriate place on his left leg.

"And the back?"

I shuffled toward a hind leg and demonstrated there as well. My hands were steady, which surprised me.

"*Ja*, good." She turned back to the audience, striking her palms together. "Next horse," she said.

Everyone was beaming away at her, utterly delighted with what they'd just seen. And I don't mean the humbling pose she'd made me assume. No one seemed to realize that if Katerina Schwetman hadn't adjusted my position at the last minute before she'd given Spier the call to do his capriole, I'd have been kicked, probably, to Kingdom come.

CHAPTER 13

I walked Spier along the driveway, letting him pause now and again to nibble at the lush green grass. I had the feeling that Katerina Schwetman knew damned well it was I who had taken the video of her stallion going through his maneuvers. I also knew that, pronto, I'd better put it right back where it belonged.

My plan was to replace it when I put the surcingle and long reins back in the truck. I would have to take my sweet old time cleaning the leather off so that I could do it during the afternoon break.

You see, I couldn't do it while everyone else was back at the arena, because then Frau Schwetman would know for sure that I had put it back.

Don't let anyone ever tell you that the criminal life is easy.

I poured a capful of Bigeloil, which is a liniment, into a bucket and then filled the bucket with warmish water. Then I sponged Spier's legs and the mark the surcingle had left where it matted down his coat. The stallion made sounds of appreciation as I did so, making me aware of the kind of horse owner Katerina Schwetman must be: an exceptional one, the kind that really bonded with the animals in her care.

So obviously she'd be upset about having a video of Spier doing his thing stolen from her.

Still, what if Spier had done his thing at Nika's? What if Manuel was right about Frau Schwetman stealing Nika's camera? What reason, other than theft, could there be for her having denied even knowing Nika?

So, even if I wasn't planning to try to have the woman placed on America's Most Wanted, I, for my own satisfaction, decided to see what was on the tape.

I put the freshly laundered Spier back in his stall, gave Plum a limp carrot, and carried the sweatshirt cum video back to the house where I could view it in peace.

No matter what the tape had on it, I decided, I would return it to the woman's truck and let the matter be. Then God would be back in his heaven and all would be right with the world.

I went into the screening room—it was like a little theater, really cute—popped the video into one of several VCRs, and stood at the massive television set before me.

Guess.

It had no knobs.

Remote, I thought. There's a remote.

Except that there were *four* of them on a little table to the right of one of the chairs.

I pressed one and a jungle rhythm began to pound somewhere to my rear.

I fiddled with it some more and got the drums to stop, but a brassy choir of trumpets replaced it. What was next? The Mormon Tabernacle Choir? I was sure, though, that way off in the arena, whatever horse was going now had just had an enormous shy.

I fiddled with some of the other remotes, and one, at least, caused the power to the television set to click on.

The screen was filled with static.

I went over to the VCR where I'd stuck the tape and I tried to listen, but I couldn't tell if the tape was rolling or not.

I hit eject on the VCR itself and looked at the cassette. There was a considerable amount of tape on both spools. I tried rewinding for about a minute, and then I went for play yet again.

The huge screen displayed what seemed a still picture. Very still. Because the camera was focused on Veronika's battered body.

I held my breath. I felt as though I would never be able to breathe again. Because the picture wasn't a still after all. There was blood moving down the side of Nika's temple, blood accruing in a pool beneath what at one time had been Nika's face.

I started pressing buttons on the remote and the tape moved forward and back erratically. I was afraid that I'd accidentally erase the tape that I had somehow to get into the hands of the Austin police.

Frantically, I searched for a wall plug and yanked every electric cord that had been plugged into it.

The television went dark. The tape ejected automatically.

And from another room, Edie's voice called, "Robin? Are you here?" This was followed by the clang of many additional voices. I strained to hear if Katerina Schwetman's was among them.

Meanwhile, I grabbed a tape from the rack—it was called *Ultimate Abs*, an exercise video. I popped this into the VCR and I stuck the tape of Nika into the cardboard box that had held it. Then I thought, No, this is too easy, and I began pulling tapes out of cartons and shuffling them all up and then putting them back at random. I closed the cabinet door just in time.

"Here you are," Edie said. "We were looking for you." Frau Schwetman dimpled in the doorway beside her. "We'll all be out by the pool. It was getting so hot, we decided to resume the clinic tonight and just veg out for now." She glanced at the plethora of remotes. "You must be going nuts trying to figure this out. Let me help you."

Frau Schwetman stepped into the room with her.

Meanwhile, Edie was squeezing and shaking the remotes. With everything unplugged, of course, they didn't do a thing. She noted that the cassette deck was up and she pushed it back down. It popped up again.

"Guess we'll have to wait until my husband gets back from Austin. This is really his thing. Anyway, he's got his client out on OR, so he ought to be in tonight."

I knew his client was Ron. "OR?" I questioned.

"Own Recognizance."

Frau Katerina Schwetman reached past Edie Conover and pulled the tape out of the machine. I watched her as she squinted at the label, *Ultimate Abs*, and then at me.

"Once a phys. ed. major," I said, though clearly she didn't know what I was talking about, "always a phys. ed. major."

"If you two didn't bring your bathing suits," Edie told us both, "I've got an assortment of them right outside in the pool house. Just grab."

Then she left Katerina Schwetman and me alone together.

"You haf, I think, the tape that is mine," she said.

"No, no, I don't have it."

"How can I be sure?"

"I don't know, Frau Schwetman, but—" In *this*

country, I thought I'd say, we're innocent, you know, until we're *proven* guilty, but I didn't have the chance.

"Silence," she said, right after I'd gotten "but" out of my mouth. She walked past me and opened several of the cabinet doors.

Videos up the wazoo. Probably a thousand videos. Even Frau Schwetman seemed daunted.

She turned back to face me just as I slipped out of the door.

I ran to the pool house, grabbed a gaudy one-piece suit, and was out of my clothes and into it and back with the others at poolside before she'd even emerged from the house. Unless she'd decided to stay in there and search.

I doubted she'd be able to find the tape, though. And if she could, well, I'd tell the police anyway. Manuel could testify that she'd been at Nika's house.

I began doing laps. The other women all seemed content with sunbathing. I did one, two, three laps in a kind of mindless way.

Then I thought that maybe I should call the police right now.

Except that it seemed odd. I mean, to climb out of the pool while everyone was lolling about on chaises and go inside where Frau Schwetman was holed up and make this call. Still, that meant the police would get to Braedock before Frau Schwetman had a chance to destroy the tape. What did I care how it looked to the others? The tape, after all, was proof. God, this was murder after all. But was it? Maybe it *had* been an accident that the camera had inadvertently caught. Maybe Frau Schwetman knew how someone might interpret the video—I mean, hadn't I just leaped to that same conclusion—and maybe that was why she took the thing. Except, then, why was she menacing me?

I climbed out. Grabbed a towel and dried myself as well as I could, then wrapped it like a turban around my hair.

I went in through the kitchen door. It closed solidly behind me. I was instantly shivering, in part from fear, in part from the air-conditioning. I went to the counter where the phone was hung.

Just as I reached for it she came at me out of nowhere. She grabbed my wrist, then released it and went for my throat. I cried out, but I doubted that anyone outside could hear.

The towel around my head began to slide and half covered my face. I reached for it with both hands just as Frau Schwetman let her foot fly.

The blow doubled me over. I began to cough. I also thought I was going to throw up. "You vill find for me the cassette," she said, grabbing my damp wrist with both of her hands and wrenching it so that my skin burned beneath her grasp.

"Okay, okay," I said, "I will."

I didn't know if anyone had used the phone since yesterday, but even before I could straighten up and stand upright, I grabbed for it, hitting redial and the speakerphone button all at once.

The little *doot-doot-dat-dat* business came blaring into the room. Frau Schwetman squeezed me harder, then squeezed on top of the squeeze as if she were punishing me for every single one of the little connecting tones.

Then: "Yes?" Jeet's one word like a beacon, steady and sure. Frau Schwetman dropped my aching wrist and stared up at the source of my husband's voice.

I choked back a sob.

She remembered the knife rack, and as I took a breath to speak she pulled the largest of the knives out.

"Jeet," I said.

"Honey, hi!" He sounded so stupidly cheerful. "How're you doing?"

A tear rolled down my cheek.

She lifted the knife blade toward me very slowly, the way a Ninja might.

"Fine," I said.

"You sure? You don't sound too good."

She smiled and kind of saluted me with the blade.

"I'm sure," I said. Then I had an idea. "You must be sick of all those grapes," I began, emphasizing the last word. "You must have grapes coming out of your ears." I began to laugh hysterically—and I really do mean hysterically. It was some insane reaction of my nervous system to the stress. "I always loved grapes," I said. "Grape was always right for me. I mean, everyone was drinking cream soda, cherry cola, but not me. It was always grape, always grape."

"You've been out in the sun again, haven't you?" He sounded dismayed.

And then I shouted, "Grapes, gra-apes, gra—"

Frau Schwetman pressed the button that cut him off. Then she lifted the knife and cut through the wire that connected the telephone base to the wall.

Her voice was so calm. "You vill find, please, my tape."

I nodded. Along with the tears, my nose was running and I kept trying to sniff it in, but I was leaking all the same. I rubbed my knuckle against my nostrils.

She let the knife blade rest against my bare back.

"Now, please," she said.

We were almost at the doorway of the video room when we heard the other women coming back inside the house. Frau Schwetman let the blade touch me again as a reminder. Then she pushed me so I'd move faster.

Believe me, I did.

Of course it occurred to me to scream, but what would that have gotten me? A huge blade right between the ribs. So I moved on.

We went outside through the entryway and ended up in front of the house. I could see some gardeners at work, but I could also hear the drone of their gasoline-powered equipment. Even if I shouted, I realized, none of them would hear.

"Look," I tried, "Nika probably deserved everything she got. I know she was blackmailing you about Melissa Song." Remembering the burned-out magazine cover Nika had stashed away made me say that. It was a long shot, to be sure.

But, bingo! Frau Schwetman grabbed my shoulder, whirled me around, and slapped me as hard as she could across the face.

I fell to one knee, stunned mentally as well as physically. No one in my entire life had ever hit me before. No one.

"Get up," she said. "And quickly, to the truck."

"Look," I said, but the minute she raised her hand to strike me again, I stopped. "Okay, okay, I'm going." I wiped the gravel off my bare knee and hustled toward the parking area. A couple of flies kept buzzing my back. I felt as though I must be bleeding there.

All the while I was thinking, What is this? I mean, I ought to be able to take her. I mean, I'm a hale and hearty phys. ed. major after all and she's—what?—a granny. Except that I didn't want her to hurt me again.

Who would have thought I'd turn into such a weenie? All I could think of, though, was how great it would be to have some knight come riding in on a charger or else have Superman come streaking down from the sky faster than a speeding bullet.

Which brought me to Jeet. Would Jeet be able to figure out that I was trying to tell him with all that business about the grapes that this involved Veronika? But Jeet didn't know where I was exactly. I mean, I'd told him Houston and I may even have told him Braedock, but he's not a horse person. Braedock wouldn't mean anything to him.

And anyway, it didn't seem as though Frau Schwetman and I were planning to stay at Braedock.

"Which is yours?" she asked, indicating the various truck-and-trailer combinations before us.

"Guess," I said.

She walked over to the dinkiest one, which of course *was* mine.

She opened the left rear door of the horse trailer and then made me lie down on the side where Plum usually stood. Which made me wish that I had cleaned it out the minute I'd unloaded the mare. Because there was a colossal pile of dung in there, dry, but still . . .

And it adhered to my damp bathing suit. And it itched against my legs.

But that seemed minor compared with what was to come. Because she tied my feet and then my hands with the longe, wrapping it around my legs and my torso and my neck.

But not my mouth!

I made up my mind that the minute she walked away I would give it my all and scream. "Help me!" I hollered, elongating each word so as to achieve maximum amplification. The metal of the trailer walls seemed to hold all of the sound in. "He-ee-elp!"

I listened, but instead of rescuers, I heard only the slam of Mother's cab.

And then she was there, Katerina Schwetman, the roll of duct tape that I kept so conveniently on my dashboard in her hand.

"Oh, please, no," I said, "I won't scream again, I promise."

"That is correct," she said, unspooling tape from the roll and wrapping it across my mouth and around the back of my head and then my mouth again until she'd used up all that was left.

I heard someone running, then Edie's far-off voice. "Did someone call for help?" I heard her ask.

Inside, on the trailer floor, I approximated an emphatic nod as well as I could.

"It was Robin Vaughan, trying to carry too heavy a load," Frau Schwetman said, her voice moving in the direction from which Edie's had come. "I helped her and now she is fine."

I was there on the dung-strewn trailer floor for hours. I ached and I itched, and I had to pee. Also, I was all cried out. I promised the Deity that if I got out of this in one piece, I would never snoop, I would never spy, I would never even be minimally curious again.

The Deity was not available for comment.

Darkness fell. The flies stopped coming and the mosquitoes started. They were like cartoon mosquitoes, making loud *n-yaar* sounds in my ear. Soon the mosquito bites began to swell and burn. Eventually I started thinking, What would be so bad about peeing with a bathing suit on?

Except that even when I tried, I couldn't. My bladder

felt huge, as if I'd swallowed something as big as the Liberty Bell.

And maybe worst of all, Edie was evidently hosting a cookout down below. I could smell the sizzling beef and charcoal and I could hear, very faintly, the tinny sound of a mariachi band playing.

Didn't anyone even wonder where I was? Or had Frau Schwetman made up some excuse?

Hell would be like this, for sure. I'd be miserable and alone, and hungry, too.

Eventually I heard footsteps. I made mmm-mmm sounds and rolled and thrashed against the trailer's metal sides, but if anyone heard me, they undoubtedly thought I was a horse protesting my confinement. I thought about banging in Morse code, but who knows Morse code anyway? Not even me.

Finally I lay still and listened.

I heard horses coming near, the soft blowing that they do. Then a nicker, a feminine one, answered by a deeper call. Plum, I was sure of it. I'd know her voice anywhere. The other one, I thought, though I'd heard it but once, was Spier.

Then the trailer door was opened. Silhouetted against the night sky was Frau Katerina Schwetman. "Good evening," she said. Her accent didn't sound German anymore, it sounded Transylvanian. I fully expected her to change into a bat and fly away.

No such luck.

She grabbed my arms and braced her booted foot against my bare toes. She yanked me upright. In addition to having stubbed five of my toes all at once, I was so stiff from having lain in one position that I almost fell over on top of her. She felt my weight lurching onto her and pushed at me so that I ended up resting against the trailer's cold metal side.

She unwound the part of the line that tied my hands to my feet. I inched my body into an upright position. Nothing in my life had ever felt better. I strained upward. I did pelvic tilts. I moved everything that *would* move. If I could only go to the bathroom, I thought, my life would be complete.

Now she jerked me out onto the ground. I stumbled and fell, and she kicked at me, rolling me out of the way. She, who had been so nice when she worked with horses!

Then she loaded them, Spier first, onto the side where Plum ordinarily traveled, then Plum herself.

Both horses were thoroughly prepared for the ride, with their head bumpers on, their legs and tails completely wrapped.

Then she leaned down and started undoing the tape around my mouth. "Ve are taking your truck," she said. "You vill not make undue noise."

I moved my mouth around, making elaborate *O*s and *E*s and then I said, "Yeah, well, I don't exactly have the keys." Her eyes said I'd better get them, and I heard myself very quickly admitting that I kept a spare in a little metal box beneath the tongue of the trailer. Frau Schwetman went to retrieve it. I couldn't resist adding, "You won't get very far in this truck of mine, by the way. It has a million things wrong with it."

She was back. "You drove it from Austin, correct? All the way to here," she said.

Well, true, but I do kind of know how. Meanwhile, I did figure out why it was *my* rig she was using and not her own. Someone had left a tractor parked in front of hers. But where was she going, anyway? And why take Plum?

But it wasn't just Plum she was taking. Because next she was holding the roll of duct tape that I keep on my dash. She was going to do up my mouth again. "Hey, wait," I said, "I really have to pee." She ignored what I'd said and applied the tape. Then she was making me lie down in the front of the trailer, and sideways, right by the horses' front feet.

Maybe she didn't understand, I reasoned, being a foreigner and all. I found I could make a hissing kind of sound underneath the tape. I did this, hoping she'd figure out that I had to pee. She seemed amused by my attempt at communication.

The horses, on the other hand, were frightened by it. I watched those huge hooves of Spier's dance inches from my face and decided that I wasn't going to hiss ever again.

She closed the escape door and seconds later, *vroom,* Mother started.

Talk about noise! The trailer rattled and shook, the metal-against-metal sound setting up a very nearly constant squeal. And, in addition, the trailer lurched and swayed. I forgave every horse I've ever dealt with for not wanting to load.

After a few minutes the trailer bounced and clattered to a halt. Frau Schwetman came around and opened the escape door. She untied me, and undid the tape that bound my mouth.

"You will relieve yourself," she said. "Then we drive on."

"Where?" I asked. I rubbed my mouth with my hands, but neither my lips nor my fingers seemed able to feel anything. It was as if I'd been given injections of Novocain.

"Here. Right here." She meant in the trailer, right where I stood.

I'm not a super-fastidious person, but I just couldn't

do it. That's not saying I didn't try. I pulled my bathing suit down and I squatted, but I'd held it for so long that I couldn't get anything to come out.

Frau Schwetman sighed, obviously losing patience. "Get out then and go," she shouted.

It was the same outside by the road. I squatted for what seemed an aeon. Just when she said, "Enough," and was about to get me back inside, the flow began. That took a long time, too.

When she tied me up the next time, she didn't use the longe. Instead she did all of me with the duct tape. This eased the bonds a bit. And she tied my hands and my feet separately. So I was a lot more comfortable in every way when I crawled back inside.

I was trying to keep my spirits up, thinking, Jeez, people pay two hundred dollars an hour to be with her; me, she kidnaps.

But it seemed a feeble joke right now.

I found myself totally unable to think of the larger picture. Instead, I focused on what would undoubtedly prove to be niggly little complaints. I had a host of these left to consider even after I'd gone to the bathroom, with more problems making themselves known every minute.

For instance, the jiggledy racket that the trailer made hadn't ever abated. Also, the horses were impatient now, stomping more and playing at eating their hay. The hay nets, of course, were hanging directly over me. Whenever the horses pulled a bit of hay free, a shower of it would fall upon me. Hay tickles when it's up against bare skin. And add to the list the fact that I was now, in addition to everything else, quite cold. I had goose bumps.

I also had this sudden insight into people who whined all the time. Maybe they whined over little things because there was one enormous one they declined to face. Like that someone had taken them prisoner and was probably going to kill them and the horse they rode in on.

The trailer slowed and I heard Frau Schwetman downshifting. I felt the rig pitch left in a long sweeping arc. We were undoubtedly on a ramp approaching an interstate. Yes, I could feel the way we were gaining speed and RPMs. The engine noise grew loud and louder still. Mother was at peak power, but in second gear. I waited for Frau Schwetman to shift, but though the revs as well as the noise increased, she wasn't doing it, wasn't pushing the gearshift lever into third.

I felt a couple little starts, as though she'd let up suddenly on the gas and then hammered her foot down hard again. And I knew then what was going on.

Mother wouldn't come out of second gear.

It happens sometimes with this truck of mine.

If I hadn't been gagged, I'd have shouted, *Way to go, Mother!*

The trailer lurched to a stop.

Katerina Schwetman, eerily backlit by the halogen lights that illuminated the freeway entrance ramp, undid me, the bonds, and even my gag. "You vill behave yourself," she said, waving a little knife and deliberately yanking on a hank of my hair.

"Or?" I dared.

She pushed me toward the cab of the truck. "Or you vill be sorry," she said.

I turned toward her. My eyes had adjusted to the dimness, though my skin hadn't to the cold. I shivered as I tried to stare her down. If a car or truck came by, I thought, I'd throw myself in front of it. I'd—

"If you try anything," she said, as if reading my

intention, "your horse will suffer for it." She evidently saw the expression on my face in response to this, because she laughed. "Correct. Your precious Plum."

As if to test my resolve, a car came up on our right flank. The driver had to slow to almost a halt to make sure he could get around us without scratching the sides of his own car. He honked and rolled a window down—to call, I thought, obscenities at us. Instead, he whistled—at me in my beachwear, I could only assume.

"You wouldn't hurt a horse," I said.

She didn't comment on my remark. "Do you know what is wrong with this truck of yours?" she asked.

"Yes."

"Then fix it." She raised her hand as if to strike me and I flinched.

What if I didn't fix it? Soon it would be morning rush hour. Anyone blocking easy access to a freeway ramp would be courting death at the hands of some crazed and probably armed Houston motorist. I'm not kidding, either.

Or else the police would spot us from a helicopter and send help.

On the other hand, the one time I was broken down and counting on the police helicopter sending a patrol car, it never did come. Instead some Henry Lee Lucas look-alike pulled over and asked if there was something he could do. I almost yearned for a Henry Lee type now. Or maybe someone more modern, a big bald guy with tattoos and a nipple ring.

"Fix the truck," she said, interrupting my thoughts.

She watched as I pulled the folding stairs from the bed of the truck. I needed it to reach the part I had to tinker with. I needed a hammer, too.

Reluctantly she let me have the hammer that I kept

in the cab for just such occasions. She stood a good distance away, however, just in case I planned to assault her with it. "Remember," she said, "what I said about that mare of yours."

It didn't seem to me she would hurt the horse. After all, she'd wrapped Plum up before trailering as if the horse were going overseas—wraps, head bumper, and all. The question was, would I take that chance?

And the answer, I realized as the auto part I was banging on moved free of its little trap, was no, I would not.

Katerina Schwetman seemed to recognize this. "Now you will drive," she said smugly.

She told me to follow the signs to the Great Southwest Equestrian Center, and I did. I kept talking to her all the while, though, trying to figure this thing out. After some nonsensical chatter, I asked the biggie. "What is going on here?" I said.

"I am keeping a late-night appointment with Melissa Song," she told me.

Melissa Song.

Maybe Frau Schwetman had planned to kill her all along.

And somehow Nika blundered onto the knowledge, mentioned it, and got herself killed.

Maybe Nika had seen Frau Schwetman in a fit of fury burning the holes in the magazine cover. And being Nika, she would, of course, try to use that knowledge. I could see Nika doing it, expecting Frau Schwetman to knuckle under the way the rest of us had. Boy, had Nika pegged this one wrong! She hadn't any notion of the vastly greater evil of her adversary.

"I don't know if they have justifiable homicide in Germany," I tried, "but here, if a person was threat-

ening you, and you, you know, just kind of flipped out
and killed them, you might not go to jail. You could
argue that they made you do it. That they were, you
know, kind of evil. Edie Conover's husband, Greenback, he could probably get you off. So why don't we
just go and talk to Edie. I mean, you don't have to kill
anybody else, you could just—"

"Be quiet," she said. "You are talking like a fool."

Oh, I felt like wailing out Jeet's name.

I drove on, but the silence plagued me. Somehow I
wasn't frightened when I talked. As if I or Melissa or
anyone couldn't die with me in midsentence. "Everybody hated Nika," I said, trying to build a sense that
we were alike, Frau Schwetman and I.

"Let me tell you what she did to me," I attempted.
Then I launched into my story of how she got me to
take her to a Luby's Cafeteria and pulled the oh-golly-
I-forgot-my-wallet trick. "She ate twelve dollars and
eighty-three cents' worth of food, counting tax," I
ranted, "and she never paid me back. Every time I
asked for the money, she had some excuse. I finally
realized that she wasn't going to pay me ever. That
she'd cheated me out of that money on purpose. That
she—"

"Veronika was a tick on the body of a dog," Frau
Schwetman interjected.

"Right, a bloodsucker."

"A minor annoyance," she clarified.

"Twelve dollars and eighty-three cents," I reminded
her.

When I chanced to look over, she was staring at me—
well, the way everyone I've ever told this story to does—
in a kind of wall-eyed way.

I took another tack. "What about the photo?" I
asked. "The one of Nika in your clothes? In the top

hat, on Spier.'' Ah, yes, the fateful photograph, the appearance of which, on the TV news, had gotten me involved in all of this in the first place.

"Veronika Ballinger. She taunted me about Melissa Song. She *demanded* that I let her ride my stallion. She *demanded* that I let her wear my clothes. You should have seen her preening in the mirror. She had me take a photograph. It was pathetic, this Veronika Ballinger dressed like a rider. She should have been riding a donkey.''

I gulped. "Then why did you kill her? I mean, you *did* kill her, didn't you?''

"I told you,'' she said, "she was not fit to ride a horse. Not a good horse. Not my Spier. And it wasn't enough, sitting on him, even walking him around the arena. No. She thought she should ride him in a show. This Veronika, she said to me that she would actually do this, ride my Spier in a show.''

She was getting all worked up as she said this. I looked across at her again, and sure enough, all the round surfaces of her face seemed to have become angles. She kept on talking. "The death of Veronika Ballinger,'' she said as if boasting, "it was an exercise, a practice. Good practice, yes.''

"The tape is still back there at Braedock,'' I said. "You can't be sure that everyone isn't watching it right now. And they've probably called the police.''

"They are watching tapes, yes, but the tapes of their precious lessons with me.'' She laughed in derision.

I was glad I'd done all the additional video shuffling. "You won't find it,'' I said.

"No,'' she agreed. "*You* will. Everyone will be asleep by the time we return from this appointment and you will retrieve the tape for me. Unless of course you do not value your own horse's life.''

Well, that answered my question about why I had been brought along. And Plum, too. It also meant, though, that she wasn't planning to kill me on any part of the present trip. I was glad about that.

Just then an animal—a skunk, I think—bolted onto the highway. I braked and swerved. Almost immediately, there was a crash behind us in the trailer. It and the truck began to shake. Frau Schwetman and I sort of looked at each other in alarm. Then, without even having to think, I pulled the truck to the side of the road, flung open the cab door, and ran back there.

Frau Schwetman did the same. She slipped in through the escape door while I stood outside on the road.

"What is it?" I asked her.

"Bah!" she said. "You have tied this net too low."

I poked my head inside. Spier had somehow managed to fling his right front leg high enough to catch it in the hay net.

Frau Schwetman was pulling at the knot I'd made, but the weight of Spier's foot only made it tighter. It was impossible to open.

"Where's your knife?" I asked her.

She patted her pockets, but she couldn't seem to come up with it.

"Great," I said. "We could be here all week."

The only good news was that the stallion was standing stock-still. Some horses will do this when they get themselves hung up. The dumber ones will throw themselves around and make matters much, much worse.

Katerina Schwetman grabbed hold of Spier's big bandaged hoof. I took hold of the net. As if we'd been working together all of our lives, I pulled and she pushed. Grunting with the effort, we managed to free Spier's foot and get it back on the floor where it belonged.

We were both out of breath, but we laughed with relief. She cuffed me on the chin, but playfully. "I will teach you to tie a hay net," she said.

But then suddenly we both became aware of the external situation again. Of the fact that I was her captive. Her face grew stern.

"Look, this is stupid," I said. "Instead of running back here to help Spier, I could have slammed the door on you, locked you in here. But I didn't. I *helped* you. Doesn't that count for something?"

"You are a person who truly loves horses, Robin Vaughan," she said. "I regret, however, that we must continue our journey as before."

I got bold. "Yeah, well, you don't have that knife of yours, do you? So why should I say yes?" Plus I was nearer to the escape door than she was.

She slid her hand across her hip. A tiny gun appeared. "I have never cared for firearms the way you Americans do," she told me. "Still . . ."

I let her march me back to the driver's seat.

"I can sort of understand about Nika," I said when we were under way again and she'd pocketed her piece, "but what has Melissa Song ever done to you?"

"It is what Melissa Song *might* do that concerns me."

That burned-out magazine cover. The story that went with it. I remembered that article. It was all about how the U.S. had never won an Olympic gold in dressage and how Germany's Schwetman twins had seemed a shoe-in until Melissa Song came on the scene. It had mentioned the Schwetmans by name.

"Oh, come on," I said. "That story was all hype. There's no way some nobody from Texas is going to outride the German team."

"Have you seen her?" Frau Schwetman asked me. "Have you seen her ride?"

"It was a couple of years ago. Training level. She couldn't possibly be ready to compete in the Olympics." Still, I remembered the way Melissa sat a horse, the way we'd all watched her, the way the scribe had risen to her feet to applaud. The scribe said Melissa had gotten an eight on rider position. I think I'm great when I get a six. But no one had seen the test sheet even though she hadn't bothered to claim it after the show. It had disappeared, like Washington's teeth and Kennedy's brain.

And now Melissa was getting all kinds of big-time publicity, so obviously she wasn't riding training level anymore. Word was that her secret sponsor had arranged some kind of audition with the honchos on the United States Equestrian Team and that when they saw her, they went crazy, too. All the rest would be history.

Still, killing Melissa seemed a bit much. But then, so did killing Nika. But hey, the Schwetman twins were the fruits of Katerina's demented womb. Some mothers would do anything for their kids. I mean, weren't we in Texas, home of the pom-pom mom—the woman who had tried to have the mother of her daughter's rival on the high-school cheerleading squad murdered?

I turned off the interstate at the appointed exit and cut down the road that led to the center. The parking lot was huge and deserted except for a lone monster truck down near the entrance to the first of the three indoor arenas up ahead.

It had a custom license plate: SONG.

"What will you do?" I asked as she reached for the duct tape yet again. "Shoot her? Hack her to death with a kitchen knife? Or what?"

She looked at me curiously. "You didn't see on the

tape? You didn't watch? Tsk, tsk, tsk.'' She continued making this sound and shaking her head from side to side in a slow, disbelieving no.

She was still tsking as she bound me again and put me right back into the trailer where I had been before. From my vantage point on the floor, I watched as she unloaded Spier. I heard her crooning to him as she took his wraps off. ''You vill be a good boy, Spier? Good, *ja*?''

I heard his huge shod hooves striking the parking lot pavement as he was led away.

CHAPTER 14

I felt those needle-sharp pains in the bridge of my nose that meant I was going to cry. I tried not to. I told myself that I'd only get my nose clogged up and then, what with the duct tape on my mouth, I wouldn't be able to breathe. Did I want to smother myself?

Hell, no.

On the other hand, I wasn't exactly brimful of alternate plans, either.

Except that, as I had at other, shall we say "crunch" moments in my life, I thought of my old gym teacher, Miss Barr. God, I didn't even know her first name. I would have to live in order to learn it. And her address, too. So I could send her flowers. Miss Barr blazed in my mind's eye like the Statue of Liberty, except that instead of robes, she wore an antiquated navy-blue one-piece gym suit, actually quite fashionable now. And instead of a torch, she had a starting pistol raised aloft.

It was quite a picture, the squat Miss Barr elbowing the Lady of Liberty off her pedestal and assuming, on stumpy legs and with a carefree display of varicosities, her stance.

I began laughing. Salt tears formed in my eyes and coursed down the side of my probably filthy face.

How would they rewrite the "Send me your tired, your poor" poem that's engraved on the statue's base?

They'd have to mention Miss Barr's favorite words. Words like "discipline" and "self-mortification."

It was Miss Barr who made us do all kinds of awful things. Like vault to a standing position from a lying-down one on the floor.

Granted, she didn't tie our hands and legs together first, but still . . .

But even as I thought of doing this I was aware of a deep and maybe even profound weakness in my arms and legs and even in my *will* as a result of all that I'd been through in the past few hours.

What was it Miss Barr used to cheer at us when we'd reached the point in a game or a workout where we couldn't possibly go on? "Are you committed?" she would chant. "Are you committed?"

"No," I would always mutter under my breath, "but you ought to be." And whoever was near enough to hear would laugh and I'd take advantage of that moment to sink the basket, steal the base, or whatever.

This wasn't going to work, I realized, under the present circumstances. Still, it inspired me sufficiently to kind of wriggle and inch my way from the front of the trailer into the compartment where Spier had been standing. Even though it was just a distance of a few feet, my shoulder and my hip, which bore the brunt of my weight as I did this, ached mightily.

In any case, once I'd gained the lengthier vertical section, I was able to do a sort of stretch, taking my legs out of fetal position and extending them down the trailer's length. This felt unbelievably good, the way, say, a tepid shower feels after you've spent the day all hot and sticky in the sun. And if *this* felt good, imagine how untying myself and actually moving around might feel.

If this were a movie, I thought, I would find something sharp to use on my bonds, or else I'd have Plum chew through them. But exceptional horse owner that I was, there wouldn't be anything even remotely sharp inside my trailer. And Plum, bless her heart, couldn't be more unconcerned. She chewed at her hay so placidly that you'd have thought I often curled up in a bathing suit at her feet.

Her feet.

I stared at them in the darkness, thinking of the tiny stubs of horseshoeing nails that protruded from her hooves.

Very tiny stubs. But still . . .

I put my hands forward, but Plum kept pulling the foot I'd reached and stomping it down an inch or so away. And anyway, I consoled myself, those nail stubs had been filed way down. I was trying the impossible. I was wasting precious time. Finally, she stopped stomping and I was able to rest my hand against her foot.

Or against her bandages, I should say. Because Frau Schwetman had wrapped that mare even better than she'd bound me.

So, curses, I was foiled again.

Okay, I told myself, what I had to do was stand.

I rolled onto my back and thought about this, thought about being flat on my back on the gym mat. Thought about rocking my legs and hips up and giving a heave and—voilà!

But did I have the strength now for the thrust it would take? The last time I had done this, I was young and lean and lithe and I hadn't lain bound and gagged in the back of a horse trailer for hours in preparation for the effort.

I flung my legs back and then forward again real hard.

I managed to gain a sitting position, but I also scared the bejeesus out of Plum.

In fact, had she not been tied, she probably would have banged her bumper on the trailer roof. As it was, she yanked her trailer tie so hard that the entire vehicle shook with her effort. At the very same moment she kicked against the trailer's metal sides. And horses being the dumb creatures that they are, the very racket she was setting up was scaring her even more. She sat back as far as the tie would let her and shook her head and neck this way and that, all the while letting those mean hooves fly.

I'm not kidding, I saw sparks when the metal from the base of her shoe connected.

And even though I knew that with the center partition in place, I was safe, it was scary to be dressed so scantily—and at the same time be so close to all that force, all that potential maiming capability.

On the other hand, I couldn't just sit here, waiting for her frenzy to subside. I had to keep trying to get out, keep trying to stand up.

I prepared myself for the major thrust that it would take to do this. Plum seemed to prepare for it, too. She was still, but I could smell her sweat and feel her trembling. In the darkness, too, I could see the flash of her wild eye. Lord knows what she thought I was doing. If I lived through this whole experience, I realized, I'd probably never be able to load her again. And she'd reached the point where she was oh, so easy.

I was just gearing up to give the leap my all when it occurred to me that Miss Barr never did let us do things the easy way. Easy, to her, had been a dirty word. But she wasn't here now, and I was being a bozo about all of this by conjuring up her memory.

All I *had* to do, I realized, was fall over the *other*

way, onto my hands and knees. I could do this without flinging myself around, too. And then standing up would be a piece of cake.

Despite my nearly locked joints, it was.

I reached out and consoled my mare, stroking with the sides of my hands and making mmm-mmm sounds deep in my throat.

Okay. I was staring at the trailer's rear doors, which were about the height of my boobs. What I had to do was leap up and fall on top of them, maybe at the waist. Then I'd at least be able to get out of the trailer.

This maneuver also thrilled my horse. I had to ignore the shaking and the banging and continue, I knew.

The third time I tried, I managed to do the first part of it. It hurt like hell and it knocked all the wind out of me, but I balanced there anyway, dizzy either from the blow I'd delivered myself across the middle or from the knowledge that I was three quarters of the way toward freedom.

Well, relative freedom.

Plum's wham-bam went on. Even so, I balanced there on the door's edge until I could breathe again. Then I dropped my head and thrust with my legs with all my might. It was like a huge ungainly dive into a concrete sea. The last thing I remember was a ringing blow as my head hit the pavement.

I was out of it, I know, because a huge ocean liner sailed by. Everyone I knew was on it. Jeet was wearing a chef's hat and blowing kisses, and Nika, dressed in organdy, was cooing at a happy Ron. Lola and Cody were getting married, and the captain of the ship, Frau Schwetman, was about to perform the ceremony.

All the bridesmaids were horses. Flowers had been braided into their manes. I had thought the shimmer on their hooves was jewels, but when they started to melt, I realized they weren't jewels at all, they were ice cubes carved to look like jewels.

I came to shaking. I was still, you'll recall, in Edie's garish loaner bathing suit. I didn't know how long I had been unconscious, but I had evidently bloodied my nose in the fall to the pavement. It had had time to bleed quite a bit before stopping. The blood had turned from liquid into sticky ooze.

Plum, meanwhile, was quiet, but the way my head felt, she might as well have still been carrying on. Indeed, I'd crossed some kind of terrible line. I mean, dying right that very minute, or at least lapsing back into unconsciousness, seemed an enormous cocoon-like lure. My eyes closed. Under my duct tape, I was probably smiling. My ship, my ship, my ship was coming in.

Then Miss Barr hurled a life preserver over the side. She was shouting, "Are you committed? Are you, girls?"

Thus I managed to get to my feet yet again.

Ahead of me was the lighted arena. Hey, I could always hop there.

But I knew I wouldn't have to. The thing is, I knew something about duct tape that maybe Frau Schwetman and the thousands of other felons for whom it is the bond of choice don't seem to know. I knew that it has all the horizontal strength in the world, but that if you rip it even a wee bit vertically, it will tear like the weakest fabric. No kidding, it's that easy.

So I hopped not toward the lighted structure, but back to the truck in search of something to tear on.

That wasn't hard. I used the edge of the front license plate on my truck. I did the hand bond first, then picked at the edge of the ankle bond, unraveling it. Then, gingerly, I pulled the tape off my mouth. Frau Schwetman had wound it at least five times around my entire head, so of course it tugged at my hair as before, but this time particularly at the tender nape of my neck.

Oh, *ouch*.

Now I looked inside the truck. Sure enough, Frau Schwetman had been stupid enough to leave the spare key in the ignition. I could drive away, I realized, save myself and Plum, too. And why not? For all I knew, Melissa Song was already dead, her own blood drying into syrup the way mine had.

On the other hand, suppose she *wasn't* dead. And suppose that if I drove off, she *would* be.

I sighed resignedly, grabbed a blanket of Plum's from behind the seat to stave off the chill, and trudged toward the huge lighted indoor.

I thought strange things along the way. Like how Ron would get off because of me. Ron, who made his wife dress up in little-girl clothes. Then I thought it was no goddamn wonder Nika was the bitch she was. No wonder she was into little power trips, little ways of lording herself over other people, with a husband who made her do things like that.

Except that, compared with Katerina Schwetman's deeds, everything Nika Ballinger had ever done now seemed small and venial.

CHAPTER 15

I saw them the minute I gained the entrance. They were in the center of the large expanse, all of which was dazzlingly lit. Spier was in his surcingle and long reins just as he'd been for the demo Katerina Schwetman had given at Braedock. He gleamed under the lights like the superstar he was. His ears were pricked, his neck was gorgeously arched. He was a thing of beauty, a joy if not forever at least for now.

The arena had been set up for something smaller than a dressage show, with rows of interlocked chairs set directly on the arena floor. As if an intimate, small-scale sort of theatrical production was about to take place.

Except that the chairs were empty. Melissa had evidently been told to come alone.

But maybe I was crazy after all. Because Frau Schwetman wasn't *killing* Melissa in there, she was, instead, treating her to the performance of her life. I could even hear Melissa Song's little squeals of pleasure. At one point a fragment of her dialogue wafted up to where I stood. "Oooh, I *really* appreciate this," she was saying.

I stood there wondering if I'd hallucinated the whole peril thing. The ache-all-over feeling that I had, however, convinced me that it had to be real.

But it did seem dreamlike as, once again, Spier began to perform the age-old airs above the ground. I stood there, awed. Levade. Courbette. And now, if his routine was the same as before, the capriole.

Frau Schwetman went through the same routine she'd gone through before. She patted Spier, his shoulder, his croup. She spoke to him and, with her hands on his very body, seemed to sense through her fingertips whether or not he was ready for the mighty leap and kick.

He looked ready. His massive body was coiled like a spring, all that energy compressing, compressing, about to let fly. Off to the side, Melissa had clasped her hands together as if trying to contain her excitement. I had felt that same rush just hours before. Spier was about to perform what, for a horse, was the ultimate feat.

Katerina Schwetman continued stroking Spier. And then, as if it were an afterthought, she looked at Melissa, looked at America's first *serious* Olympic-gold-medal hopeful, this tiny but ferociously talented girl, and she crooked her finger as she had to me, as in, "Here. You will take the reins."

Melissa went through all the gestures I had gone through, the disbelief, the do-you-mean-*me*? And then she hopped forward just as I had, not about to miss the opportunity of a lifetime.

And all at once—don't ask me how—I knew exactly how Veronika Ballinger had died. I knew because I'd stood there, right there where Melissa was about to stand, right in the spot where those massive hooves of Spier were set to fly.

What had Katerina Schwetman said about Nika's death? An exercise, a practice.

And they were about the same height, Nika and Melissa. The blow would catch somewhere in the vicinity of the eyes. The bridge of the nose, maybe—wasn't that some ancient killing zone?

I held the horse blanket high up over my head so that I wouldn't trip on the straps and buckles that dangled from it, and I ran down the aisle, down the steps that led to the center of the arena, screaming, "Stop! Stop! Stop!"

I scared the hell out of Spier, who bolted, long reins streaming behind him. He made for the row of chairs, and Frau Schwetman was running behind him, frantically trying to grab or step on one of the long leather lines to regain control.

Melissa Song was pointing at me with a look of utter horror on her face. I guess it was the blood from my nosebleed all over my face or something, I don't know.

Spier crashed into several of the seats, the sound of splintering wood and metal mingling with the sound of Katerina Schwetman calling out his name. Still, the stallion was spooked but good and he continued his frantic attempt to escape.

He barreled through a row of seats, miraculously keeping the long lines free, and came directly toward me.

Frau Schwetman saw his intention and ran toward the bottom of the aisle to halt him if he turned. And turn he did. He took one look at me, or maybe at the blanket, and he did a pirouette that would have earned him a fifteen out of the possible ten that you get in the Grand Prix test.

With a giant leap, he bounded toward his owner, who stood at the base of the aisle with her arms outstretched.

I thought he'd stop. Horses do that, career right toward you full tilt and then—*screech!*—they chicken out and turn into lambs as they let themselves be caught.

Katerina Schwetman evidently thought the same

thing. But he didn't stop, he didn't even slow his pace. He hit her head-on, running flat out. It was like being hit by a bus. Frau Schwetman landed maybe thirty feet away from the collision site thanks to the force of Spier's blow.

The impact seemed to do the stallion in. He stood snorting, his wet body gleaming in the light, steam rising in waves from his body. His sides heaved.

Frau Katerina Schwetman hadn't fared as well. She was conscious, but her eyes seemed unable to work as a pair. Fluid—blood and a kind of serum, trickled from her ears and her nose. She was trying to speak but only rasping. Her left arm jerked and danced as if it had a life of its own.

Melissa Song was nowhere in sight.

I knelt over Katerina Schwetman and put Plum's blanket over her. I was just tucking it in around the shoulders when, suddenly, behind me, Melissa appeared after all. "Move and I'll shoot," she said.

I tried to turn my head and my neck sort of wouldn't. I moved the entire upper half of my body toward her voice. Yup. She somehow had Frau Schwetman's tiny gun. It was aimed, two-handedly, at me. I turned back.

"I've called the police," Melissa said. "And nine-one-one. I don't know who you are, but don't you move."

Frau Schwetman began rasping out words. It was as if she were answering Melissa's question about who I was. "Robin Vaughan," she said, "Robin Vaughan." At least I think that's what she was saying. It was hard to tell.

But deep in my heart I knew why Katerina Schwetman was calling me. I knew what she wanted to know. I knew it the way only a fellow horse lover would. So the first thing I said to her was, "Spier's okay. He's stopped running and he isn't cut or lame or anything. He's okay."

Tears welled up in her unfocused eyes. I touched the crown of braids in her hair and then tears welled up in mine. Her hand continued its odd jerking motion.

Melissa still had the gun trained on me, but now she didn't look nearly as resolved. She looked from me to the horse, as if she'd only just now realized that maybe instead of threatening me, she ought to be doing something for him. But for all she knew, *I* was the nutcase. I was the one who was responsible for Frau Schwetman's injuries.

Frau Schwetman's lips began to move again, and she made dry little sounds in her throat. I leaned over and Melissa also came in close.

Until now I hadn't been afraid of Melissa or the gun. Now, close up, I looked at its sleek black barrel and felt a brand-new tug of fear. I didn't expect Melissa to shoot me in cold blood, but hey, accidents can happen.

She was still holding the gun with two hands, the way cops do on TV. Weren't her hands getting tired by now?

"Robin Vaughan," Frau Schwetman croaked.

Melissa dropped her hands, held the gun now at her side.

Frau Schwetman went on. Both her eyes seemed to be aimed at me now, and I took it as a good sign. But at the same time they didn't look as though they could see. They were dimmer, glazed, as if her batteries were running down.

"Did you hear me, Frau Schwetman?" I yelled. "He's okay. Spier's okay." I ignored the gun and made my way over to where the horse was standing. This time he didn't run.

I pulled at his long rein and brought him to her side.

I stood there patting him and talking louder than was necessary about how absolutely wonderful and fine he was.

Frau Schwetman's head lolled up and down as if she were agreeing. Then, with a voice that sounded as though it was bubbling in her throat, she said, "Robin Vaughan, I give you Spier." Finally, except for that awful flailing hand, she went limp.

We heard the helicopter as it came in. I ran out to the lot to meet it, but was driven back inside by the swirl of wind and pebbles that the rotor raised against my skin. I could see my trailer moving and I knew that Plum was terrified again, what with the engine noise and all that debris being showered on the trailer's side.

She'll survive this, I told myself, wishing I were there to lay a comforting hand on her shoulder. I silently thanked Frau Schwetman, too, for the wonderful job she'd done wrapping my horse's legs.

Then I watched as the medics ministered to Frau Schwetman, strapping her onto a long board and clamping an oxygen mask down over her face.

Despite their attention, it turned out that "I give you Spier" were the last words that Katerina Dreiss Schwetman, three-time winner of the individual gold medal in Olympic dressage, ever spoke.

CHAPTER 16

Melissa lent me a pair of sweats—they stretched sufficiently to fit me—and helped me settle Plum and Spier into stalls beside her own horse. Then she drove me to Ben Taub Hospital, where Frau Schwetman had been taken.

"She's probably in intensive care or something," I advised. "If anyone asks if we're related to her, say yes, that we're her daughters, Thea and Nan."

Melissa knew the names of the twins, of course. She nodded her head, but she smiled.

I hadn't had any idea what Melissa was going to say about me to the police, but when they came, she didn't tell them anything about me and my part in the accident, the way my running down the aisle with the blanket had spooked Spier. That hadn't, after all, been my intention.

But she absolutely would not buy my story about how Spier was going to lift into the capriole and knock her dead.

"I know this sounds even more bizarre," I told her, "but I think I have a videotape of him doing it to someone else."

The idea of letting the charges that had been lodged against Ron Ballinger stand briefly flickered across my mind. Well, of course I wouldn't do that, but it was kind of tempting. And for all I knew, he *had* deliberately kept from calling 911 on the off chance that he could thus free himself up for Suzie.

Such a world.

We walked into the hospital to learn officially that Katerina Schwetman was dead. Somebody said something about calling the German embassy and then somebody else handed me a plastic bag.

Inside the bag was Frau Schwetman's watch and, right down to her knee-highs, the clothes she had worn. I found myself wondering if the riding breeches—they were stretch, after all—would fit me. And then I thought about Nika wearing that FEI stuff, the shadbelly and the canary vest and the top hat, and I shuddered. Maybe I could just get the clothes bronzed or something. Never actually put them on my person.

I dug around the bag some more. And—oh, God, I was about to become one of the people I've made fun of all my life but—*mirabile dictu*, all squashed up but *there* was the two-hundred-dollar check I'd made out to the Frau.

"Can you run me over to Braedock," I asked my new friend, "or else take me back to my truck?"

"I'll take you," Melissa answered. "I want to see this alleged tape."

We tried creeping up the Braedock drive in the predawn gloom, but Melissa's truck, a super-cab dually— you know, 4 wheels on the rear instead of two—that was lit up like a Vegas nightclub, was hard to miss. I had expected the big old manor house to be dark, but it was lit up, too. No kidding, lights on all the floors. I had forgotten that these people got up even before the chickens do.

But anyway, before we even reached the house, we

almost ran down Edie, who was striding, like an angry apparition, down the drive. She came right over to me on the passenger side.

I rolled my window down.

"Where have you been?" she shrieked.

I thought she had been worried, but then she said, "And how dare you lure our clinician away? And how dare you invite all those other people? They just came pounding in, waking up the entire house."

"Lure?" I repeated. "Did you say 'lure' ?"

"I'm really angry," Edie said. "I'm sorry that I let you come." She still hadn't looked at the driver's side, still hadn't noticed Melissa.

"Edie," I began, "I didn't lure anybody. And your clinician isn't coming back."

It was then she saw Melissa Song. Fortunately, around this time a dozen others began streaming toward us, Jeet and Lola and Cody in the forefront of the knot.

I leaped out of the truck and ran to intercept them.

Jeet wrapped his arms around me and said, "Oh, thank God." I leaned against him so completely that I thought we'd both topple. Everyone seemed to be asking me something, but "What happened?" seemed to be the question that prevailed.

I pulled back from Jeet for a moment, looking for Melissa. I made a frantic *Shhh!* sign at her just in case she was planning to speak. I mean, now that I owned this fantastic stallion, Spier, I didn't want someone deciding he was a killer and taking him away. I didn't want her to mention the tape.

Of course, without mentioning the tape, the whole thing would sound really goony. Because without mentioning the tape, I had to eliminate the Veronika Ballinger part, making it seem as though Frau Schwetman had kidnapped me for no good reason. Unless, of course, no one believed that she had kidnapped me to begin with.

"Let's go inside," Jeet told everyone as he scrutinized the expression on my face. "I have a feeling this is a very long story."

I started out by telling them Frau Schwetman was dead. I swear, if Melissa Song hadn't been there to back me up, no one would have believed even this. Then I backtracked. "It starts with Veronika Ballinger," I said. "With her death."

"Not so loud," Edie whispered. "Ron Ballinger and his girlfriend are upstairs."

"Upstairs!" Lo and I chorused.

"He's my husband's client," she explained. "He's out on bond."

"Go get your husband," I told her. Then I went into the tale.

The clincher was the videotape, which, after endless fumbling with one cardboard video holder after another, starting with *Ultimate Abs* and ending with *Sunset Boulevard*, I was finally able to stick into the machine.

We all watched it, watched the demonstration we had seen right here the day before, Spier doing his thing. And there was Frau Schwetman behind him, whip in hand. *"Ja, ja."* There was the old pat on the rump, the "good boy, Spier."

I held my breath. Beside me, I could hear Melissa holding hers. Spier gathered himself, as ready as he'd ever be. And then Frau Schwetman gestured to someone out of the camera's range.

Veronika Ballinger strutted into view. She wasn't doing what Melissa had done, what I had done, the thunderstruck *"Moi?"* that the moment called for. Oh, no. She was swaggering, heady at this, the ultimate power trip.

Here she was, a girl who'd grown up under a freeway ramp, lording it over an international riding star.

I think Katerina Schwetman saw all that and hated it completely. I think it probably cemented her resolve. Because what came next was uglier than anything I could have imagined.

Spier. Just Spier. He bursts up into the air and his legs flash out behind him. That fast, and he's back down. Katerina approaches to congratulate him. Then she looks directly into the camera lens. I swear, if she'd have had a mustache, she'd have twirled it.

She walks toward the camera, then disappears. Then the lens jerks to another view.

We all gasp.

There is Nika, her face ripped in half. You can't even tell that she has eyes. And there's that bloodstain, spreading. And everyone in the room, every one of us, understands that Katerina Schwetman is now filming this, filming the deceased, on purpose. Katerina Schwetman has captured this moment, up close and personal.

Edie or someone hit a button, freezing the frame right there just as Ron, yawning, opened the door and came into the video room. "Oh, Jesus," he said, his voice thick with emotion. Suzie bounced in, saw the screen, and without looking away or altering her gait, came to Ron's side. She was wearing saddle shoes and knee socks and she had a great big pussy bow in her hair. She linked her arm through his and dropped her head on his shoulder. My stomach lurched.

I turned to look at Lola, but her eyes were riveted on the screen.

I looked at Melissa Song. She was staring at the ugly image, too. She had her hands up, her fingertips resting on her cheeks. Clearly, she believed my story now.

Ron reached around behind the television set and yanked the plug. "I think we've seen enough of this," he said. His voice was thick and sorrowful, the way it had been when I'd talked to him on the phone. So maybe, despite everything, he'd cared about Veronika a bit.

"Oh, hi, Mr. Ballinger," Melissa chirped.

"Hiya, kid," Ron said.

"Mr. Ballinger is my sponsor," Melissa explained. "He's been footing all my bills for three years now."

Ron seemed embarrassed. "Anything for a good cause," he said.

Suzie raised her eyebrows and put her hands on her hips. She glared at him.

"It got Veronika's goat," Ron said. "I liked doing that, okay?"

"Ron and Veronika. Just your average, everyday suburban couple," Cody provided.

Greenback broke in. "Well, it won't get Edie's goat if I take up where you left off," he said.

"Not at all." Edie patted Melissa's arm and then her husband's, too. As an afterthought, she walked over and patted mine. "I'm sorry I was rude to you, Robin, when you first drove up. I'm really glad you came to the clinic," she said.

Yeah, me too.

Jeet leaned toward my ear. "I meant to tell you. That was good thinking, babbling about those grapes," he said. "That's how I finally figured out that you were in trouble."

I could picture him in his room down on Padre complaining to the photographer, demanding to know why I, Robin Vaughan, wife of a goddamn food critic, would say Véronique when I ought to have known that spinach would be Florentine? "But that wasn't all," he went on.

"Right," Lo said. "Because then, to check it out, he called me and I'd just finished talking to Wanda. She'd come running over to the house, practically hysterical, something about your aura."

"What was it?" I asked. "Plaid?"

"Worse. It was polka dot. No kidding, it was purple with big black blots and she said that your absolute essence was being threatened."

"Yeah," I said, "that sounds about right."

"We just stopped everything"—Cody winked—"and drove on down here."

Lola blushed. That was when I realized that Cody had probably been at Lola's when I'd said I was coming right over and she'd brushed me off. What a bozo I'd been, thinking even for a minute that she had somehow been suspicious. Now I made up for my lapse by envisioning the sign Lo had shown me, LoCo Farms, at the end of their driveway. Yes.

"Let's get out of here," Jeet said. "Get your horse, okay?"

I looked at Melissa.

"Well, uh," I said, "my horse isn't exactly here."

"Wherever," Jeet said. "Let's just go get her."

"Well, uh, it isn't exactly *her* anymore," I said.

Melissa was whispering in Lola's ear, presumably filling her in on this aspect of the story.

"What do you mean," Jeet was saying, "it isn't *her* anymore?"

"It's uh, sort of *them* now, Jeet."

"*Them?*" he was shouting. "You want me to believe that Plum, out of nowhere, had a baby?"

"This isn't a baby, Jeet, it's, uh . . ."

Everyone in the room was looking at me. Melissa

stepped in my direction. "Just before she died, Frau Katerina Schwetman gave her stallion, Spier, to Robin. I witnessed this," she explained to the room at large.

"Katerina Schwetman *what*?"

Jeet wasn't the only one in the room who said this, but he was the one who said it the loudest.